D1520038

Iron Peter

A year in the Mythopoetic Life of New York City

a novel by
Charles Ortleb

Rubicon Media
New York City

Iron Peter: A year in the Mythopoetic Life of New York City

Published in the United States by Rubicon Media, P. O. Box 1823, Radio City Station, New York, NY 10101-1823

Copyright © 1998 by Charles Ortleb

All rights reserved under International and Pan-American Copyright Conventions. No part of this book may be used or reproduced in any manner without the express written permission of the publisher, except in the case of brief quotations contained in critical articles and reviews.

Publisher's note: This novel is a work of fiction. Names, characters, and incidents either are a product of the author's imagination or are used fictitiously, and any actual resemblance to actual persons or animals, living or dead, events, or locales is entirely coincidental.

The text of Iron Peter can be purchased on the Internet. An electronic version is available in Adobe Acrobat Reader format from Electron Press at www.electronpress.com.

First Rubicon Media Edition: June 1998

10 9 8 7 6 5

PRINTED IN THE UNITED STATES OF AMERICA.

Library of Congress Catalog Card Number: 98-91325

ISBN: 0-9663454-0-1

Iron Peter

A year in the Mythopoetic Life of
New York City

This book is dedicated
with gratitude
to
Francis,
Neenyah, Tom, and Ray

and in memory
of Fran Bradshaw
the golden woman
who waved a wand
of humor and
understanding that
healed everyone
in her path.

There is something fascinating about a man's
being inviolable, untemptable, unswayable.

Hannah Arendt
Men in Dark Times

Overture

Peter was dressed in red and black when he arrived in the overwhelming snow of Christmas 1995. Veiled in white, Manhattan startled him. It looked like the storybook image he memorized in childhood. There were carolers in nineteenth-century costumes on one of the street corners he passed on his way to his hotel in the West Forties.

As the dark descended and the giant snowflakes obscured their vision, strangers paused to feast on Peter's magnificence. Suddenly, with Peter's figure thrown into relief against the accumulating snow, the city was transfixed in a mysterious moment of deep eroticism. Peter's path left an aroused chain of men and women. But mostly men.

They need not have doubted the reality of what was before them. This was the most beautiful man they had seen in years. Maybe decades. This vision hurt some and left scars of envy. But it also healed and inspired and sent prodigal bodies back to the gymnasium. Some would end up in bed that night, their minds in a dither as they searched the slide show of their day for that timeless face, that knightly body and that amazing blond hair on the capless wonder.

For some of them, Peter's presence was validation of the most important decision they had made in their lives. They said to themselves, "This is why I live in Manhattan. If I ever think of leaving this city, may God strike me dead. This is the greatest city in the world."

It was New York's lucky day. As the golden young man moved in his own uniquely passionate rhythm, through the graceful waves of snow, he could have been a cosmic gift come to place himself beneath the big voluptuous Christmas tree at Rockefeller Center, in the city of AIDS.

1996

January

His presence at the hotel caused quite a stir as he brushed the snow from himself and his bags. My, my, what has Santa brought, thought the hotel's manager as he passed Peter in the lobby. Some of the employees immediately suspected that he was a new soap opera star, but if so, what was he doing here? Had there been a fight with his girlfriend—or boyfriend? There were some bets, derived from a little wishful thinking, that he was in town to do underwear ads for Calvin Klein. The big question for every person who saw him was, why is he alone?

As Peter stood at the registration desk, a hush fell over the lobby as if it were suddenly the vestibule of a church. The bellhops wondered if they should offer him any help with his bath. Did he want any extra towels or condoms?

After Peter had unpacked and showered in his room on the top floor, he called his father at his logging business in the West to tell him that he had arrived without incident. His father expressed great concern that his son had made a terrible mistake in coming alone to New York. He reminded his father that he was a man, which always surprised his father when it was put to him that way, for Peter had always struck his father as some astonishing, vulnerable creature from another planet. If Peter's father had ever found that his son were made ill by kryptonite, he would not have been surprised.

After mutual expressions of love, and after his father made him promise that he'd call if he needed anything, Peter hung up the phone, and with tears in his eyes, went to the window and stared out into the snowy static that filled the air around the nervous traffic down on Eighth Avenue. Jesus, I'm really here, he thought. I did it.

Why had this amazing young man come to New York City? He didn't have a single friend or relative here. He had no immediate career prospects. He was but a lowly English major with a minor in Bible studies. He had no intention of starting in a mailroom on Wall Street or in the entertainment industry and making it to the top. He could have been a model or an escort in the blink of a gay eye. No, he had come here because Manhattan had something that he could not find anywhere else in the country to the degree that he could find it here. New York, the financial and intellectual capital of the world, had AIDS. With a young man's dreams and passions, this golden lad had come to New York City to stalk AIDS.

If you wanted to stalk AIDS, you could try Chicago or Los Angeles or San Francisco or Detroit or Boston, but that would be big AIDS in a small pond. No, Peter didn't want his life to be second best. He wanted Big AIDS in the Big Pond. In the cosmology of AIDS, it was where the Big Bang of AIDS had occurred. If he could find it here, he could find it anywhere.

If anyone in the government had known why Peter was in Manhattan, a law would have been found under which he could have been put on the first train out. But one could still arrive anonymously in the Metropolis and be given the benefit of the doubt. Not that Peter had bad intentions. No, it was just that beneath his pulchritude lay an agenda that none of the city fathers or mothers would have embraced. Peter had come to New York to assassinate the AIDS epidemic.

Like any astute assassin, Peter intended to case the joint very, very carefully. Unlike most assassins who do everything to avoid drawing attention to themselves, Peter arrived in the city like a barge full of fireworks. Peter was an assassin who hid himself in plain sight.

In order to assassinate AIDS, Peter would have to immerse himself totally in what was loosely called "the gay world." Every evening, Peter found his way into a different bar in the city like a member of a gay militia visiting federal buildings. He launched his attempt to understand every part of the AIDS Empire.

With a gay guide in his pocket, he began in the hotel's neighborhood, where the gay bars were dark and smoky and filled with men who seemed mummified by cigarettes and alcohol. The smiles he saw in the bars often looked like they had been painted on by a mortician. Bars were frequently lit so that you couldn't distinguish the living from the dead.

He sat for a while in the ennui of Cat's Bar looking at aging

5

gypsies, and then he headed down to Cleo's on Ninth Avenue. He taxied down to Chelsea and made the rounds to Barracuda, The Break, and finally the bar in which he would become something of a legend: Splash. In January, Splash was still one of the hippest places in town, and as the temporary gay Capistrano, it was where the most beautiful men migrated. When Peter walked in, the competition ended. Golden Peter ruined the night, every night, for many a gay man.

Peter created a crisis in the gay kingdom because he was made of a material they had never seen: total unavailability. Of course, these men had experienced distance and unavailability in their lives, but never this total. Had they not grown up in the straight kingdom? Had the spiffiest of them not experienced the occasional rejection? But Peter's total unavailability was a kind they had never known in their lives. Peter was the price they would pay for swearing allegiance to the AIDS Empire. They had become its citizens and its defenders. The space around Peter was like a treacherous moat that encircles an enchanted castle. Every knight in the bar secretly wanted to cross it.

As Peter sat sipping a martini or soda water in bar after bar, his eyes would pan the room, looking for the telltale signs of the AIDS Empire. Every bar had some poster or a fake work of art that was in reality AIDS propaganda. There was in every bar an advertisement for an AIDS dance or marathon or walk or bike ride or bare butt stage show benefit, all to raise money for that universally admired cause, AIDS research, prevention, and education.

Throughout that cold and windy first month of 1996, Peter trekked from bar to bar checking out the floor plans of gay life in the AIDS Empire. He would be the archaeologist and anthropologist of the dying world he was determined not to enter. At least not yet. Peter wanted to hear the stories that these men told each other about the plague. Their eyes glazed over whenever the subject of AIDS came up, as if they were in a trance. Perhaps the keys to the trance lay hidden in their tales.

His father had given him more than enough money to live comfortably for a couple of months before he looked for employment. He was not worried about finding a job. People usually didn't want him doing things for *them*. They wanted to do things for *him*.

6

The employees of the hotel watched in amazement as Peter returned alone late every evening after his investigative forays. To their dismay he was always by himself. He never satisfied their curiosity about what he was into. Was this a young man who had suffered some bizarre injury, perhaps in gymnastics or on the high dive, one which had deprived him of the physical possibilities of sexuality? Perhaps he had a rich eccentric father who had taken him on a dangerous wild boar hunt and there had been an unseemly accident. Was he planning on having a gender reassignment? Whatever it was, what a waste!

And they wondered, what the hell does he do in his hotel room? Does he stare all night at the golden god in the room's full length mirror? If ever there were a ravishing young man that they could imagine falling in love with himself, it was Peter.

They would never guess that, alone in his room, Peter was pure anger. He transformed himself into a dark brooding creature of the forest. He stewed and he boiled. From his window he raged at the moon and snarled at the stars. What had been denied him because he swore he would never sleep in the plague's bed of lies? He should have been ascending through life like a swan on the wings of Eros with Streisand hamming it up in the background. This was his precious time-sensitive youth and night after lonely night, no one would caress and adore it. These were the days and weeks and months when memories were supposed to be created. He developed the furious obsessions of the true assassin.

The epidemic would pay for this.

That January Peter saw *Victor/Victoria* on Broadway and he felt very sorry for Julie Andrews. He spent many of his early afternoons at the movies. He saw *Leaving Las Vegas, Sense and Sensibility, Persuasion, Muriel's Wedding, Carrington, Get Shorty, Mighty Aphrodite, Casino, When Night is Falling,* and *Heat.* One night he went to the cabaret at the Cafe Carlyle to see Eartha Kitt. Miss Kitt seemed a little annoyed during her performance because every time she began to purr at her audience, she could not help but notice that many heads were turned to the back of the room where Peter sparkled alone with his martini.

Peter's evenings were devoted to AIDS. Peter wanted to see

how AIDS was hardwired in the gay psyche. In bar after bar he met men who revealed the dark secrets of the AIDS Empire. The gay bars were full of the masters of the erotic hunt, but somehow they had lost the wilderness they were born in. Peter met every kind of hunter. He made the acquaintance of dominant white males, tit lovers, Long Island chubbies, older gays with big arms, horse hungs, naughty, passion-filled submissives, Batman mentors, leather Asians looking for spankings, Harlem body-builders who were versatile and kinky, horny jocks, beefy butches, skinny butches, feminist skinheads, cigar lovers, dildo servicers, older professors, younger professors, and bores.

Many of the men told Peter that they had shaved the hair off of their chests, not that it mattered to Peter. He thought, no wonder many of them seemed so insubstantial. They had removed the animal part of themselves that connected them to the earth. Peter wondered if they let a few hairs grow around their genitals for old time's sake. Many of the older ones seemed to be used up boys trying to make their way back in time by doing facetious things with their faces, their hair, and their clothes.

Peter disappointed each of them, but he seemed to arouse something deep in every single one. He listened to them in a way that made them think that no one had paid serious attention to them before. They seemed to be suffering from a dreadful lack of real respect and concern. Peter talked to them like they were important in ways they had never considered. The hunger that Peter saw in their eyes wasn't just for his beauty. They seemed to be reaching out for something essential that had disappeared from their lives. They weren't just looking for missing childhoods or parents. They were looking for a lost world and they didn't even know it.

Peter tried to find out as much about each man as possible, but mostly his questions were about their relationship to the AIDS Empire. What did they think was really going on? What were they doing about it? Were they afraid? Did they really believe everything the government had said about the epidemic? The more questions that Peter asked about the AIDS Empire, the more powerful the magnetic field around him became. His suitors all hopefully suspected that he was sizing them up to see if they were safe for the night's finale. They kept waiting for him to ask them that last touchy question which had become a form of foreplay in the gay community: their HIV status. But he never did. Like Boy Scouts with the most important and difficult merit badge, they were all extremely proud of their HIV status. For some, it was like being a member of Mensa.

Peter's visage was mercurial. Like all great eye candy, he had many alluring faces and people tended to see the one they wanted to see. Peter brought out the spontaneous generosity in gay men. Accountants wanted to do his taxes. Singers wanted to belt for him. Lawyers offered to sue the world for him. Fashion designers were ready to design speedos just for him. Bankers wanted to open their vaults. Taxi drivers were ready to drive him to Provincetown for the weekend, gratis.

The bars were Peter's bestiaries for the taking. He could have just snapped his fingers and hypnotically turned any of his mesmerized audience into venereal tigers, seals, dolphins, doves, or dogs. Peter could have had any material possession that Manhattan had to offer. But what he wanted was something none of them seemed to have either the brains or the courage to give. There was not a knight in this gay kingdom who could or would valiantly destroy the AIDS Empire.

One young courtier, thinking that he spotted a streak of civic responsibility in Peter, used a humanitarian pick-up line to zero in on his prey. He told Peter that he had volunteered for a sociologist's study of HIV-negative men which he had been assured would help end the AIDS epidemic. The scientist was trying to uncover the relationship between body types and the risk of HIV infection. Every Thursday the young man went to a university on the Upper West Side and sat in a room full of other concerned HIV-negative men. When his name was called he went into the scientist's office, where he was asked to undress. He was then photographed for a half hour in a variety of positions. Even though he thought it was strange that the scientist was wearing a Hawaiian shirt and Bermuda shorts, the young man was clearly thrilled to be making a contribution. He didn't know exactly how, but the doctor had assured him that it was a very important study that would hasten the end of the epidemic. All the participants in the study had been given striking AIDS activist T-shirts that said "Please forgive me for being HIV-negative."

When the young man finished the story, he looked like he expected Peter to praise him.

"I don't sleep with retarded gay guinea pigs," Peter said.

The young man looked devastated. Here he had shown his ability to sacrifice himself for the good of all mankind, to offer himself up to cutting-edge medical science, and one of God's cutest angels had mocked him.

Peter really loved to dance in the bars. His dancing had fierceness, daring and wild inventiveness. He danced as though he had been nurtured by music all his life and he related to it as if it were a lover's body. There was so much energy in his dancing that one couldn't tell whether he was longing for explosive sex or the fight of the century. Peter loved watching gay men dance because their bodies said something that their voices did not: that deep down they were all desperately longing for freedom from the AIDS Empire.

Men who spoke to Peter in the bars were always amazed by how much Peter knew about gay current events. None of them guessed that Peter was a voracious reader and that he was as political as he was beautiful. And while all of these men lived in the gay kingdom, few of them seemed to know what was really happening in their world.

If any of them had wanted a lover with a photographic memory, they had targeted the right quarry. Peter clearly read all the gay magazines and newspapers. To talk to him was to tune into the gay nightly news. That January, Peter took each man on a magic carpet tour of the gay reality they were ignoring. He told them that in Israel's Knesset, one religious lawmaker was arguing that homosexuality is punishable by death under Jewish traditions. In New York City, the Board of Education was voting to promote abstinence education and halt condom distribution. A saliva test for HIV infection was nearing approval by the Food and Drug Administration. In California, legislators were passing legislation outlawing gay marriage. In Georgia, where the venerable Centers for Disease Control was indeed controlling everything that everyone knew about AIDS, the state attorney general was defending his decision not to hire a lesbian. An Indiana School board passed a resolution denouncing homosexual activity. In Michigan, a man nearly lost his job for admitting he was gay. In Los Angeles, a man claimed that he was fired from his law firm because he was HIV-positive and gay. In Montgomery, Alabama, a federal judge upheld a decision by an Alabama prison to segregate prisoners who were HIV-positive. In Texas, a Christian group organized a boycott against companies that advertised in a gay publication. In Houston, neo-Nazis stabbed a gay man 35 times after telling friends that they were going to get a fag. Depending on whom he was talking to, Peter would end this litany of news by saying "Courage, gay courage!"

Not everyone liked the fact that Peter knew so much about what was going on. Behind his back, one catty gay man referred to Peter as "her highness." Men in the bars often tried to pull Peter's masculinity out from under him. It was fun. It was gay male feminism.

People looked at Peter as though he were a Ken doll with a microchip. And Peter looked back at them as though they were the hand puppets of the AIDS Empire.

During the morning hours, Peter toured the city looking for the historic gay sites that he had heard discussed as if they were the Old World by the gay men at his university. He looked for the spirit of his forebears at the Oscar Wilde bookstore, the Stonewall Bar, Sheridan Square, Christopher Street, the infamous piers, the gay cruising area of Central Park. Everywhere he went in the gay kingdom, he saw the propaganda of the AIDS Empire. It was not the cosmopolitan paradise he had fantasized about as a child. The Big Apple had a giant poisonous worm inside it.

The Times Square he had heard so much about was disappearing behind the fences of construction sites. The dust of moral fervor was in the air. The evil people of 42nd Street were disappearing into the sewers where they would be devoured by the ancient species of alligators that swam in the city's vast underground network. A cultural war had taken place here and sex had lost, perhaps temporarily, perhaps forever. Passion was retreating to new hiding places on the borders of the city and trying to open up new beachheads in the outer boroughs. Peter wondered if an invisible Gettysburg of the erotic had transpired here. The battlefield casualties seemed to be mocked ironically by the huge billboards of groups of handsome and buffed young men at play in the manner of all young men, in their briefs and boxers. At 43rd Street, Peter felt like he was standing at the crossroads of a contradiction. Sex was simultaneously everywhere and nowhere. This was a very strange Empire.

Peter especially liked wandering along Manhattan's waterfront. It was only his third week in Manhattan when he happened to see a dead man for the first time in his life. Around noon one day Peter was peering into the cold dark water off the pier at the foot of Christopher Street. A curious crowd had gathered and they were stunned by a body that was repeatedly surfacing and sinking, as though the dead man were dancing to his own house music beneath the waters. When the bloated but weirdly smiling face reached the surface of the water, there was a peculiar golden glow to it. The man had long hair that seemed to stretch to the bottom of the river. The crowd was speculating about whether the drowned man had fallen or was murdered. Peter was transfixed. He shuddered and felt light-headed. What if this were the only man in New York who had what it took to be his lover? Who knew? A frightened part of him recognized that he had come to a very perfidious place to do a very dangerous thing.

Among the cultural events that Peter could have partaken in that January was a heated debate by gay leaders about who was persecuted more, gay men or lesbians. The African Ancestral Lesbians United for Societal Change were holding their own Kwanza celebration. In SoHo, Progressive Culture Works was presenting a show about the urgent questions of gender identity in America. If Peter had wanted to go into gay law enforcement, the New York Police Department was holding a forum at the Gay and Lesbian Community Center to increase the presence of gay men and lesbians on the New York City force. And in the unimaginable event that Peter wanted to become a volunteer in the AIDS Empire, he could have had his pick. There were organizations as far as the charitable eye could see: The Mid-Hudson Valley AIDS Task Force, the AIDS/HIV Support Group at Grace & St. Paul's Church, the AIDS Center of Queens County, The AIDS Treatment Data Network, The Health Education AIDS Liaison Group, The Long Island Association for AIDS Care, The National Minority AIDS Council, the Staten Island AIDS Task Force, The Women AIDS

Resource Network, and The Women's HIV/AIDS Support Group. The list stretched to China.

Peter had heard that the city was inundated with AIDS propaganda, but the reality and sheer density of it overwhelmed him. He found it in every kind of gay venue. No one had protected the borders of the young gay kingdom. The AIDS activists had overrun the entire realm. There were AIDS posters and AIDS flyers and AIDS newspapers in every gay health club, movie house, theater, restaurant, bar, and bathhouse. Also all over bus stops, subways and taxicabs. New York City looked like one big AIDS prevention campaign. This was not the New York of Billie Holiday, Frank Sinatra and Jimmy Durante. Attila the AIDS Hun had been here.

All the signs and posters drove home the same message. HIV is the cause of AIDS. HIV is *certainly* the cause of AIDS. HIV is *absolutely* the cause of AIDS. A night didn't go by at the bars when Peter didn't hear this message peppering conversations. This truly was the virus that protested too much. No sooner had two men introduced themselves than they were pledging allegiance to HIV, the virus that causes AIDS. One night, in one of his mischievous and impious experiments, Peter loudly referred to HIV as the virus that causes gas and the whole bar fell into horrified silence.

AIDS solidarity was everywhere. The solidarity of frightened, deceived and comatose souls.

One night in the Village in the middle of the month, a sad man in drag who had been wearing a red ribbon and carrying a Teddy Bear with a golden tiara suddenly walked up to Peter and handed him the bear. He told Peter to give it to someone with AIDS. Peter left the bear on a stool at the bar, hoping someone would buy it a drink. People were always spontaneously offering him things that he didn't want.

Their bodies, for instance. At a very dark tavern on the Lower East Side, a very intense East Village AIDS activist in a Silence = Attitude T-shirt approached him and used the world famous East Village seduction technique.

The man petulantly whispered into Peter's ear, "I want to fuck you with a condom."

"I'd rather vote Republican," Peter responded.

The man's face fell. It resembled Martha Raye's in her final years. Peter stared intensely at the man, taking his measure. The obnoxious man looked like all the other activists to Peter. He stood there gasping for air like a living, breathing gargoyle. Someone had waved an evil wand at the city and all those bizarre, macabre ornaments had come alive and separated themselves from old buildings all over Manhattan. They invaded and infiltrated gay life. They had erected the AIDS Empire. Some of them resembled enormous rats and others resembled delirious trolls. New York had been overrun and infested. What would it take to return these miserable AIDS activists to the building facades and dark nooks and crannies beneath New York's bridges? Who would perform the necessary magic against the AIDS Empire?

Peter was very quickly developing a nasty little reputation among the AIDS activists. He may have been the most devastatingly beautiful man in New York, but he was seriously flawed. He lacked something. He needed AIDS awareness and AIDS education, big time. And many of the activists longed to give it to him through what they called "direct action." Preferably in bed.

Little did they know with whom they were messing.

Peter wondered, on what deadly assembly line are these activists being constructed? One after another they approached Peter with their irresistible activist insouciance, and one after another they burned their little activist fingers and discovered that Peter was not the recruitable gay boy next door. Wherever Peter went, he seemed to ruin the sexual ecology of bars. What was an uncooperative mind like that doing in such a golden body? It was unnatural.

One rather emaciated man in his thirties became obsessed with Peter at Charlie's in the Village. He was desperate. He approached Peter, introduced himself, and told Peter that he had sold his life insurance policy and that even though he had just seen Peter for the first time, he wanted to spend it all by taking Peter to Key West. He would spend all his AIDS treasure on Peter. All Peter had to do was accompany him south and let the man look at him drinking pina coladas while the sick man took his AIDS medications. Peter didn't have to do anything, not even take off his clothes.

That was unusual, because men were always trying to find excuses for Peter to take off his clothes. They invited him to bath houses, underwear parties, private orgies, and nude gallery openings. People who didn't know how to operate cameras invited him to model for them. Peter always had the perfect response. He told them that out of sympathy for all the people who had died of AIDS, he was not taking his clothes off in public until the epidemic was over. They usually clutched their red ribbons in awe and disappointment. He sometimes went further and tortured his acolytes by saying, "How can you have sex when people are dying?" They turned away from him in shame. This truly was an extraordinary young man. Meanwhile, he was afraid that if he touched any of these guys he would immediately turn into an angry winged creature made of stone and cemented onto a high rent-stabilized floor above Manhattan. Peter wanted to open every cage in the AIDS Empire and set gay men free from the gargoyles.

There were no petitioners he had more fun turning down in the gay kingdom than AIDS doctors. One evening at a bar as Peter was reading the *New York Messenger*, he was approached by a man in his late thirties who was extremely handsome himself. He had clearly decided that Peter's looks were on a par with his own and felt a sudden sense of royal sexual entitlement about Peter.

"Why are you reading that irresponsible paper?" the doctor asked.

Peter just stared at the man. He wanted to savor the moment.

When Peter didn't respond, the man said, "I know how dangerous they are because I'm a gay doctor."

When Peter *still* didn't respond, the man said, "I asked the bartender in this place not to carry that crazy rag. I thought we had put them out of business already."

Totally exasperated, the doctor said, "Do you by any chance have any hearing loss? You know that can be the first sign of AIDS. I can help you if that's a problem."

Then Peter let him have it. "Kill anyone with AZT today? Which medical cheek do you want me to kiss first? Is it Dr. Thing or Dr. Miss Thing?"

"I really like your face, but I don't really like your attitude," the doctor responded.

Peter snapped back, "My attitude is my face."

For the AIDS doctor, this was a traumatic gay experience. It only made him hate the *New York Messenger* more. And it increased his glee when later that evening, he saw a pumped-up AIDS activist dressed completely in black, slip into the bar and, after looking both ways, seize the entire pile of *Messengers*. Through the dark bar windows the doctor could see the young man dumping the *Messengers* in the trash bin outside.

The young AIDS activist didn't really have to worry about the bar's management catching him, because under pressure from some of the red-ribboned customers, the management sometimes threw the papers out themselves.

One morning back in the beginning of January, Peter had gone to a newsstand on 57th Street to search for something he had heard rumors about at his university in Colorado. People seemed to lower their voices and bow their heads in shame when mentioning it. Did Peter know that there was a local gay publication in New York City that was so controversial and so hated that it received bomb threats and was boycotted by all of the AIDS activist groups?

"Tell me more," said Peter. "Why would gay people want to destroy a gay publication?"

Nervously, because he was talking to the best-looking guy on campus, the other student said, "Because it says that the government is lying about the AIDS epidemic."

Peter felt weak. His legs almost buckled under him. The student grabbed Peter, to steady him. He was quite excited to have an opportunity to touch Peter.

"What is the name of that newspaper?" asked Peter.

Again, lowering his voice as though their conversation was being taped, right there in the middle of the main campus boulevard, the student whispered, "The *New York Messenger*."

"Yes!" said Peter. "The *New York Messenger*, the *New York Messenger*, the *New York Messenger*. Yes, yes, yes!" He was jumping up and down.

"Can I have a date?" the young man asked, thinking that he and Peter might have just bonded.

"No," said Peter. "But I love you for letting me know. I will always love you for telling me this." He was still jumping.

"Well, I guess I love myself for telling you this," the young man replied, disappointed.

That night, Peter just kept saying the name over and over to himself, like a Tony who had just found his Maria. "The *New York Messenger*, the *New York Messenger*, the *New York Messenger*. " Peter went to sleep counting *New York Messengers*. Now it was clear where he would go when he graduated. There was no question. To Peter there was nothing more important than AIDS. There was nothing more unbelievably threatening than AIDS. His soul was headed east. He would move to the capital of the AIDS Empire and the home of the *New York Messenger*.

In his four years at college, he had come to feel like an atheist among fundamentalists. Although he was not a scientist, he had taken enough courses in logic and science to smell it. The AIDS story just had an insidious stench about it. At first, he had trouble putting it into words. Peter was a creature of intuition and every alarm in his young body went off when he was around the subject of AIDS. From the minute that he first heard the acronym, whenever the word "AIDS" was uttered in terror and reverence, he had the exact same feeling he had when an aunt or an uncle, underestimating his sophistication and intelligence, began to tell him a long and winding tale full of what he in his adult years would refer to as "bullshit."

From the minute that Peter bought his first copy of the *Messenger* in New York that January, no one could say that this was a dysfunctional, ravishing young man without a companion. Peter took the *Messenger* into his life and he gave it everything that every eligible and not so eligible man in Manhattan was looking for from him. He read the *Messenger*, he talked to it, he ate with it, slept with it, played with it, went to the movies with it, cried with it, and laughed with it. Every night when he got home from the AIDS Empire, it was like returning to the faithful arms of a lover. At night, he dreamt about it. In some dreams, the *Messenger* morphed into a man even more beautiful than Peter. Finally, Peter had found something in the gay kingdom that he could trust.

Every afternoon, throughout the rest of January, Peter hiked over to the New York Public Library, checked into the microfiche room and read about the AIDS Empire in old issues of the *Messenger*. He caused the usual stir among the librarians. They had never seen someone as stunning as Peter check out a book, let alone come in and read old issues of a newspaper that some of them resented even subscribing to. One librarian had compared carrying the *Messenger* to carrying literature on how to make explosives. If they had known that Peter was an assassin, they would have been even more alarmed.

People would walk by the microfiche reader where Peter was seated just to take quick dips in the Bahamian blue pools of his eyes. And his eyes would open wider and wider as he looked at AIDS through the lens of the *Messenger*. If anyone else had muttered so much to himself, one of the guards would have asked him to keep it down, but Peter's librarians were equally enthralled by the bedroom sound of his voice. "Jesus, Jesus, for God's sake," Peter would mumble as he traveled back in AIDS time through the old issues of the *New York Messenger*.

"Why does he keep saying 'What a crock, what a crock?' " one curious male librarian asked a female librarian.

"Well, he *is* reading the *Messenger*!" was the response.

"That's all he ever reads," said the male librarian.

"Maybe he's doing a paper about Delusion and Denial in the Age of AIDS," snickered the female librarian.

Peter was indeed saying "What a crock, what a crock," at the terminal, but it was not about the *Messenger*. Through the *Messenger*, Peter felt like he had finally found the essence of AIDS.

At the microfiche reader he was like a rich kid at Christmas. He didn't know where to begin. The *Messenger* satisfied Peter's cosmic hunger. It was the stranger you bring home who strikes you as someone who has always been in your life. One who automatically knows where the bath towels are and which side of the bed is his.

The *Messenger* confirmed all his intuitions. That HIV was not the cause, that gay men were not the only victims, that a much bigger epidemic was being cruelly hidden from the American public, that all of the toxic treatments that were being rushed into the bodies of AIDS patients were actually hastening their deaths. That those at the very top of the AIDS chain of command were dishonest, bigoted and incompetent. One was more homophobic than he was crooked. Another was dumber than he was homophobic. Another was more dishonest then he was stupid. In the body of nearly every AIDS researcher there seemed to be a used car salesman trying to get out. The *Messenger* published the words that

Peter had longed to hear from a lover and friend and comrade throughout his lonely nights in college. Peter was convinced that he was living in a land of lies, and the despised *Messenger* made him feel like he was not alone.

Every day Peter floated out of the library. He felt like he had been nourished by one of those great food groups of the Bible, grace itself.

At night, as he checked out each new bar in the city, full of the gleanings of the day's reading, Peter was trailed by admirers, but no admirer dared call Peter what they called the *Messenger*: paranoid and crazy. No one sneered at Peter the way they sneered at the *Messenger*. Gay noses did not point skyward, even though this splendid creature, day after day contained more and more of the essence of the *Messenger*. No, Peter's beauty was like a crucifix. It protected him from many of the AIDS Empire's activists.

Most of Peter's wannabes could never look him in the eye and attack him. They could only deflect their rage and attack the *Messenger*. So in his own small way Peter was now making things even worse for the despised little publication.

If the *Messenger* can see what's going on so clearly, why can't these gay men, Peter wondered. These guys don't need the pantsdown spanking that some of them crave. They need a good slap in the face and a nice bucket of very cold water. They all need to be grabbed by the shoulders and shaken till all the red ribbons come tumbling off of them like leaves. Where was their longing for the truth? Had the batteries in their souls run down?

That January, at the bars, Peter could hear so many of them caught up in fatuous discussions on the legalization of gay marriage. Did they prefer to be persecuted as couples rather than as singles? Why couldn't they all see that they had been sentenced by the AIDS activists to one of the ugliest pre-arranged marriages in history? In a secret diabolical ceremony they had been married to a medical police state that the activists were building all around them.

As Peter interrogated the denizens of the gay monde and demimonde, the underlying problem became clearer and clearer. Most of the men, of all ages, while not afraid to cross a crowded bar and assault Peter with the hoariest of come-on lines (Why aren't you smiling?), risking nuclear putdowns (Because I'm fart-ing or Because God is dead), were surprisingly terrified of science. Totally terrified. Science was a fate worse than AIDS. Most of them would rather die of AIDS than try to fathom any of the details of the epidemic's multi-layered scientific fraud.

Most gay men were used to leaving medical and scientific matters to techno-nerds and "experts." Gay men did the AIDS Empire's hair. They designed the Empire's clothing. They wrote the Empire's mediocre novels. But AIDS science was both beneath them and above them. They wanted nothing to do with it. It was that wretched high school course down the hall taught by the farmer who picked his teeth with a toothpick during class while going on incomprehensibly about oxygen, hydrogen, and which cheerleaders had the biggest tits. Did scientists know whether Liza Minnelli was on or off the wagon? Could scientists properly marinate a leg of lamb and match it with the right red wine? Did they have an educated thing to say about supertitles at the opera? These gay men didn't want to go back down the hallway, clasping their books to their breasts gay-style, to re-enter the dungeons of Chemistry and Biology. They had fulfilled those curriculum requirements in a state of existential dread and had gotten on with their liberal arts destinies as quickly as possible. And yet the medical "experts" who were all too willing to take their friends and lovers, one by one, in boxes to family cemetery plots, hailed from those yucky science classes down the hall.

There were nights when Peter thought there was not one scientific bone in the gay body.

Throughout January, the one thing that the gay men Peter met in bars (except the doctors) had in common was that they all made it clear, over and over, that they were not doctors.

"I'm not a doctor," said the young poet who was taking the highly toxic DDI, "and neither are you."

"I'm sorry for daring to speak on the subject of AIDS," responded Peter. "It's true. I am a mere mortal. I'll try to confine my conversations to Fire Island and bronzer."

"I'm not a doctor," said the lighting designer to Peter, "I have to listen to the medical experts."

"You don't *have* to listen to anybody but Sondheim," rejoined Peter.

"I can't start medical school now," said a cake decorator who was still taking AZT and was beginning to look a little like Freddy Krueger.

"If just one AIDS researcher would leave science to study cake decoration, think of how many lives would be saved," responded Peter.

Night after night in the crucibles of gay life Peter could sense a palpable faith that the scientific Messiah of AIDS was coming. He was probably working in Washington at the National Institutes of Health. He might even be one of the scientists that the wacko *Messenger* attacked. One day all the hairdressers and stage managers and sous chefs would wake up in their apartments, go to the front door, pick up their copy of the *New York Times* and discover on the front page that one of the mysterious men in charge of AIDS had finally done it, made the great stroke of genius, found the magic bullet. And they would believe it because it was in the *Times*. It might even be one of those bad boys of AIDS science who had a flair for fraud. People just needed to have faith in their scientific leaders. Gag me with a spoon, thought our golden boy.

Some gay men seemed to think that they were junior members of scientific research teams because they were taking experimental AIDS medications. Peter wondered, are they all brain dead? Was the gay universe ending before his very eyes? Was this another inexorable moment in the dark history of the sacrificial lambs? Was he in a time capsule? Had he been transported back to the Middle Ages and were gay men now biomedical flagellants?

One bitterly cold night at the Eagle in Chelsea, Peter saw a sign with a hand-drawn picture of a man's face below "WANTED FOR GAY ROBBERIES." It warned patrons about going home with "a scraggily white male in his 40s, 5'4" to 5'6" tall, weighing 140 lbs. with salt and pepper hair." The man had assaulted or robbed several of his pick-ups. As he stared at the rather handsome thief, Peter fantasized replacing the drawing with the faces of the top AIDS researchers and writing: "WANTED FOR THE DEATHS OF 250,000 GAY MEN."

On the final frigid day of January, Peter walked down to the Village to visit the gay and lesbian community center. He looked through all kinds of multi-cultural gay and lesbian and bisexual and transgender literature that was on a rack on the first floor. He found one flyer that especially alarmed him. It reinforced his ominous feelings about the future. The flyer advertised an 800 number which gay people were supposed to call to be part of "A Gay Census." The ad read "As Lesbian, Gay, Bi and HIV-positive Men and Women, We Are The People Too! and We Will Be Counted!"

I bet we will, thought Peter.

February

It was the month of love and the United States of America was sending all kinds of valentines to gay people. Senator Phil Gramm, who was running hard for president, accused presidential candidate Steve Forbes of favoring policies allowing butch gays in the military. In Washington, the House of Representatives voted again to discharge members of the military who were HIV-positive. In Virginia, Governor George Allen proposed that the state housing commission ban home loans for gay and lesbian couples. In Iowa, the legislature wanted to pass a law allowing hospital workers to perform HIV tests on corpses (without the permission of the corpses) under "certain circumstances." The Director of the Illinois Department of Public Health was considering creating a central registry of people who were HIV-positive. South Dakota passed a bill banning same-sex marriage, as did California, Washington, and Iowa. In a court in Florida, a jury was deciding whether to award a child to a lesbian mother or to the father, who was a convicted murderer. In Idaho, a school board was deciding whether to force students and teachers to disclose the fact that they were HIV-positive.

Peter decided that his money could be stretched to March before he had to start looking for serious work. He had decided to try waiting on tables because that would be flexible enough to allow him to continue formulating his game plan for the assassination of the AIDS epidemic.

Throughout the month Peter explored the best that gay culture had to offer. He saw a show called *Muscular Buttbeef For Sale* at the Duplex. He went to a musical-in-progress called *My Boyfriend Looks Like Jesus* at A Different Light Bookstore. In the spirit of gender detente, he tried to go to a lesbian dance in the Village, but he was not allowed in, even though a few of the secretly bisexual women were immediately attracted to him and wanted to make him an honorary lesbian. At a theater space called The Kitchen,

Peter saw a performance of *I'm Just a Big Nellie Fruit in a Dress, and I Love It*. Gay life is wasted on the gay, thought Peter.

The month of erotic desperation brought Peter an especially hard-driving group of suitors from all parts of the gay genetic and behavioral spectrum. He met men who were into footplay and massage. He met a man who had a fetish for suit ties, dress shirts, and expensive business shoes. He met his first pec puncher. A steady stream of sensitive bottoms seemed to flow in his direction. This month, eternal fidelity meant that every one dropped promises of total monogamy in their sales pitches to Peter. And absolutely everyone was "safe." The tops, the bottoms, the middles. Some promised Peter that the sex would be so safe that there would even be a physician in attendance prepared to do a medical intervention if there were an accident. More than ever it was clear to Peter that the demons of the AIDS Empire were frolicking in the gay psyches of New York.

Seeing so many attractive men getting turned down by Peter emboldened the members of Girth and Mirth, a gay organization for chubby gay men and their admirers. Peter enjoyed talking to many of this heavy set. For a while it chagrined the gym bodies to see Peter in animated conversations with a wall of male obesity. For some reason, the rotund ones seemed more attentive and responsive to what Peter was telling them about what was really happening in the epidemic. If truth-starved fat gay men eventually began to be openly rebellious against the AIDS Empire, it might have resulted from a single effective conversation between Peter and a few bright chubbies in a single dark bar (with a free buffet) in Manhattan.

Because Peter was so manly, brusque and direct in the manner that he used to describe the government's cover-up of the Plague, men into verbal humiliation made a beeline for him. If he wasn't used to continuing his tough little act in bed, he was an excellent candidate for a quick course in VH.

Peter quickly became a subject of grave concern in the AIDS activist community. Wherever he went, Peter was the center of attention and the things he was saying were getting around town. Every gay man in Manhattan was separated from every other gay man by no more than three bartenders or two bouncers. It was the fastest grapevine on earth.

At the bars people studied Peter and tried to stand like him, move like him, and talk like him. People were repeating Peter's disturbing remarks about AIDS as though they were lines from a Terrence McNally play. All the hard work the AIDS activists had done was being threatened by this golden prince with the mouth. And what a mouth it was. Peter had never felt freer in his life. He was really flying. He said everything that he felt without fear of reprisal. He was not unaware of the unique freedom that extremely attractive people have, if they choose to use it. It seemed to him that in the gay kingdom most beautiful men were never challenged to use their mental powers, if they had any. Small talk from an A-list hunk was Pulitzer material in this milieu.

The AIDS activists went into emergency mode when the word "genocide" started popping up in bar conversations all over town. They didn't have to go far to find the source of the trouble.

Peter first referred to AIDS as "genocide" in Dick's Bar in the East Village. From there word spread to the Crowbar on East 10th Street that the most beautiful man in New York had called AIDS "genocide." Then word traveled to the Wonder Bar and then the news flashed all the way uptown to the Asian gay bar, Club 58, the virtual United Nations of gay gossip. "Genocide" henceforth spread in all directions: to Mike's on West 14th Street, to Rome and Spike in Chelsea, back down to Boots and Saddles in the Village, and then, ever so dangerously, to the unstoppable cabaret circuit. Even people who needed people were hearing the words "AIDS" and "genocide" in the same sentence.

In the cramped dressing room at Marie's Crisis, just before she was about to go on, a concerned drag queen who was taking AZT with her White Russian was informed by a drag colleague that there was a spectacular looking young man who had virtually seized control of gay society and the nouveau sensation was insisting that AIDS is "genocide." "Mon Dieu!" screamed the drag queen. And it didn't stop there. Somehow word eventually jumped the great cultural divide and reached the lesbians in Crazy Nanny's and Cubbyhole. Peter didn't have a notion about what was happening, but not since the Astor's famous ball had someone begun to arrive so dramatically all over New York City.

The AIDS activists were mortified and shaking in their Doc Maartens. They turned all the colors that AIDS activists turn. Some

25

of their faces turned the color of their ribbons. Others turned white with rage. They were truly the whitest white men in Manhattan. They had worked so hard to keep certain unpleasant questions from being raised by gay men throughout the Empire. They had struggled for over a decade to make sure that the public was educated to see reality the way that they saw it, the way the Empire demanded people see it. And now this punk, this pretty boy (this little fag, some of them actually said) was threatening a decade of intense, angry AIDS activism.

"He's got to be stopped," said one of the angriest AIDS activists.

After thanking the activist for sharing his rage, a second AIDS activist upped the ante. "He's murdering people!" the activist shrieked.

A third AIDS activist chimed in: "Now, don't upset yourself. It might interfere with your medication."

"Which one?" said the first and angriest AIDS activist.

"All twenty of them," said the second and slightly less angry AIDS activist.

The activists began a campaign aimed at taunting and intimidating Peter. But they had picked the wrong young gay man. Peter had something that most of the people who were frightened by the AIDS activists did not. He had golden balls. Peter was a beautiful, highly desirable young man full of passion who could not make love in this Empire and these AIDS activists were part of the reason. Just let them come.

They sent in their first gay brigadier.

One evening at Charlie's, a snippy little queen with purple hair in an AIDS activist T-shirt and a nose ring that had snot on it stormed up to Peter and, in the most annoying piquant voice heard since the untimely demise of Truman Capote, screamed in his face: "Where's your red ribbon, hot stuff?"

"Up your stupid, little, twisted ass. That's where it is. Be gone Miss Satan!"

The bite-sized purple AIDS activist fainted dead away and had to be carried out to the street for air.

Thus, the first maneuver in the campaign against Peter came to a crushing defeat. Was it possible that the AIDS activists had finally met their match?

The activists were facing trouble on other fronts. Peter was heartened by an article that he happened to see in the *New York Times* Sunday magazine. A young woman who had recently graduated from college wrote that she did not trust what the government was telling her about AIDS. Terrified of the disease, and terrorized by public health officials, she had constantly been tested for HIV at college even though she doubted the veracity of the official story about the epidemic. She complained that heterosexuals were repeatedly being told that they were at risk for contracting AIDS even though it seemed to her that heterosexuals who didn't sleep with dangerous drug users or bisexuals were not at risk. The woman seemed to fancy herself an expert at recognizing bisexual men and was convinced that she had slept with none. (Peter imagined a game show on which women competed for prizes by trying to pick out the bisexual men in a line-up.) Peter was thrilled to see a member of his own slacker generation finally doubting the government. But if it was lying about the heterosexual risk, what else was it lying about? The young woman seemed to have her own unique system for separating government lies and government truth the same way she was able to distinguished between bisexual and non-bisexual men. She had decided that the government's dishonesty about the epidemic came down in her favor. The government was lying, ergo she was not at risk. Why couldn't she see that if the government was lying about heterosexual AIDS risks, no one knew what was truly going on. All bets were off.

Peter need not have gotten excited about the impact of the article, because there was none. The government's AIDS experts and the AIDS activists had the public debate totally under control. The woman's doubts about AIDS were a mere hiccup and the public discourse would continue on in exactly the direction that the AIDS Empire had chosen. This chess game was being played by professionals.

Peter was especially wistful on Valentine's Day. As he walked toward the public library, he looked like the kind of creature for whom such a day was created. Every drama teacher in America would have cast Peter as Romeo. And yet there he was, alone and wrapped up against the wind, cardless, flowerless, chocolateless, loverless, and nookieless. Walking along 42nd Street, Peter was a painful sight to women alone on this most ardent of days, for what woman does not take Valentine's Day personally?

In the melancholy of the afternoon he read the *Messenger* at the library and studied the path of Dr. X, one of the celebrated AIDS researchers who had helped bring about this situation. The *Messenger* had reported on the strange homophobic behavior of Dr. X. He had blamed Fidel Castro for sending his "diseased homos" to America. That's how Dr. X had initially described the origins of AIDS. Dr. X was obsessed with the idea of people sleeping with African green monkeys and sheep. That was also responsible for AIDS. Someone had done something in bed with a bisexual green monkey or a promiscuous ewe that Dr. X had never tried and the plague of the century had been the hangover. This was the man that the AIDS activists wanted the President to appoint as AIDS Czar.

The endless AIDS activist demands that the President appoint an AIDS Czar unnerved Peter. If a national emergency were declared by an AIDS Czar, did that mean that everyone had to don long black coats, menacing boots and big furry Cossack hats? The ultimate wet dream of the AIDS activists seemed to be for the President to go on television and declare some form of martial law. What *did* these activists really want? Did they want the medical troops to come in and invade gay bars and take everyone off to far-flung parts of the newly expanded federal prison system and force them to take AZT and sing AIDS campfire songs? Did they want some special forces unit to crack down on unlicensed blowjobs all over America?

Peter stopped at a newsstand and, with only a copy of the new issue of the *Messenger* under his arm for companionship, he headed back to the hotel. Every restaurant he passed was filled with couples engaged in the conspicuous consumption of love. He felt the chill of what could have been that night. Maybe some day after the AIDS assassination there would be a Valentine's Day with a lover for him.

There would be no going to the bars that night. He lay in his bed staring at the ceiling and feeling a profound sense of loss not just for himself, but for the victims of this hideous situation. All over the world there had to be people like him who had given up the only love life they would ever have because of AIDS. In the isolation of their bedrooms they were telling themselves that it really didn't matter. There are more important things to be doing than making love. And of course they would be lying to themselves. His heartache imagined their heartache and he felt like he was channeling the sadness of the whole planet.

He tried to cheer himself up by reading the *New York Messenger*. A story about a virus called HHV-6 captured his imagination.

From what Peter read in the *Messenger* it appeared that, despite everything the government was telling the public, the virus HHV-6 was probably the real cause of AIDS rather than HIV, the darling of the AIDS activists. The only political problem for the government was that HHV-6 was not confined to gay people the way the virus HIV (with its unbelievable behavior) was. HHV-6 was not a gay virus in the manner that HIV had been advertised. HHV-6 was not the deviant virus that only slept with gay men. You could not build a crypto-fascist AIDS Empire around HHV-6. It was the uncooperative virus that colored outside the lines. If it was the real cause of AIDS, it meant that one could believe nothing the government had said about AIDS. Nada.

Much of what Peter had heard about AIDS at college had not sounded logical, and what it lacked in logic, AIDS activists seemed to make up for with repetition by constantly referring to HIV as the virus that causes AIDS. It was the Orwellian retrovirus. It had practically been chanted into existence. Just keep saying it's the cause and it becomes the cause. And keep saying that anyone who disagrees is nuts. Every time you asked a serious question about HIV you got a dismissive response: because the retrovirologists say it's so. The more old *Messengers* Peter read, the worse the situation appeared. This has got to be the biggest most murderous scam of the century—no, the millennium, thought Peter.

At the end of the very gay month of February, the police apprehended a man in the city who had been accused of defrauding AIDS patients. The man had passed himself off as an AIDS caseworker. He charged AIDS patients a special fee to get them into hospices. The man would put on an act and become the lover to some of the dying men in order to get them to sign domestic partner agreements so that he could claim all their property when they died. There was something for everyone in the AIDS Empire. Everyone except Peter.

March

If you were a boxer in March of 1996, the New York State Athletic Commission wanted to start testing you for HIV. The commission didn't want your physical safety in the ring compromised by other boxers who were secretly dying of AIDS while breaking your nose.

If you were an openly gay priest in New Jersey, you might have been receiving hate mail accusing you of committing crimes against nature. (Peter wondered if that meant that shrubs and bushes could serve subpoenas.)

If you were a gay teacher in Massachusetts and you came out to your students, you might be sued by the parents for causing emotional distress. Did parents know what algebra could do to one's emotions?

Idaho announced that, if you were gay and married to your partner in any state in the union, it would under no circumstances recognize your relationship, in case you even cared. You didn't retaliate. You still ate *their* potatoes and fortunately, gay people were still allowed to eat potatoes in all fifty states and the District of Columbia.

The big harbinger of things to come was, as usual, materializing in Texas, that great bull pen of warm-ups for America's future. A far-thinking state district judge ordered an HIV-positive man who had been arrested for car theft to inform every one of his future sexual partners in writing that he was HIV-positive. The court was kind enough to provide the man with a stack of forms for his partners to sign. The document certified that the person having sex with the HIVer knew that the potential sexual partner was infected with HIV and might be asymptomatic for Acquired Immunodeficiency Syndrome. The judge got the inspiration for the punishment after a friend's son died of AIDS. AIDS funerals always brought the best out in people. Peter thought that the judge should have been flown to New York to receive some kind of lifetime achievement award from the AIDS activists. This was a man who had a sense of urgency about AIDS. A potential AIDS Czar.

In the first week of March, Peter found a waiting job after walking around the city and looking for a restaurant where the waiters did not wear red ribbons. He also did not want to work for a restaurant that had any AIDS benefit signs in the window. Peter spotted a cute little French place in Hells Kitchen called Angel's Bistro and he went in and asked if there were any jobs. When Angel Rivera saw Peter and heard that he wanted a job as a waiter, he suspected that his mother's novenas were finally paying off. He thought, I don't even care if this one steals from me.

For the most part the interview consisted of Angel staring into Peter's blue eyes and taking deep breaths. It was more like Peter was interviewing Angel. Peter asked why the waiters didn't have red ribbons on and Angel, despite fears that Peter was an undercover AIDS activist, said nervously, "Because I think the AIDS activists are a bunch of shitheads." He was waiting for Peter to leap out of his chair when Peter said, "Sir, I think I would like to work here."

Angel told Peter that usually he had people act as busboys and food runners for a while before they became full-fledged waiters, but that he was going to make an exception and graduate Peter immediately to waiter. Peter told Angel that he wanted to learn all the ropes. Angel told him not to worry, that he would take care of all the ropes. Peter would do just fine.

Peter was up to the spiritual challenge of waiting on tables at the French bistro. He was attentive and careful and fast. He didn't spill things. He remembered the specials. He folded the napkins perfectly. He never got checks wrong. He could pronounce the names of all the wines, which many of the customers made him do over and over while they studied his face. Peter cheerfully did all the boring tasks that had to be done at the restaurant while the other waiters tried to look busy or important. Peter would even go into the kitchen sometimes and help wash the dishes which annoyed Angel because he didn't want Peter to ruin his hands. They were now part of the restaurant's assets. Peter also liked to help in the food preparation. He enjoyed peeling vegetables and preparing salads. The kitchen help was amazed. They were used to being looked down upon by the actor-dancer-model waiters.

While Peter waited on the customers, it was as though Angel was waiting on him. He attended to every one of Peter's needs. Peter had to tell Angel continually that he was being too nice, that he should not be afraid of acting like a boss. The impact on Angel's Bistro, which had been hobbling along financially, was dramatic. Nothing redistributes power in the restaurant community like a spectacular new waiter. The place turned into Lourdes. Angel could have started serving week-old food from the local deli's recycled salad bar and the bistro would still have been a hit.

When customers walked into Angel's Bistro and saw Peter, they were electrified. At first the other waiters were jealous, but since the tips were pooled, self-interest won the day. Peter was a gold mine. He was making everyone at Angel's Bistro rich. Angel thought he had won the lottery.

Peter was able to support himself with what he earned in three days of tips, and Angel let him make his own hours, so his waiting job did not interfere with the assassination planning he needed to do.

Because Peter was working, he didn't have much time to survey the gay arts and leisure scene, but he did cram in a few choice events. At the Gowanus Arts Exchange in Brooklyn, he saw an evening of lesbian musical performance and he also caught a multicultural lesbian poetry event which was sponsored by a group called Men of All Colors Together. It was Women's History Month and Peter celebrated it by going heavy on the lesbian stuff. He wanted to go to a meeting of the mother's group of the African Ancestral Lesbians for Societal Change, but he was afraid he would not be welcome. He did attend a rummage sale of extra large women's clothing to benefit a group called Fat Is a Lesbian Issue. He was not allowed into a meeting of a lesbian S/M fetish group called the Lesbian Sex Mafia.

In support of the Gay, Lesbian and Bisexual Veterans of New York, Peter attended their annual dance at the Center and danced with one of each. He also got down to the Butch/Femme Society Dance at the Network. It was black tie only.

Peter almost ruined the March 9th meeting of the Gay Men's Opera Club, which was devoted to the discussion of the largest tenor voices ever heard. All anyone wanted to talk about was

Peter's ideas about the opera. They didn't care if he had any. They just wanted to hear him talk. Peter skipped their Maria Callas discussion night, but he later heard that there was a vicious fistfight and that CDs were thrown in faces.

Peter went to a comedy club that was having a contest to find the funniest gay or lesbian in New York. The manager of one of the comics sat at Peter's table and bought him drinks. When the man asked him why he wasn't laughing, Peter told him that he thought that most of the gay and lesbian humor was flatfooted. The man sheepishly agreed with him. "Why don't you have a contest for the wittiest AIDS activist?" Peter said. "That crowd is a laugh a minute. You know, like did you hear about the one about the condom and the farmer's daughter? I mean here's a group of people that goes into St. Patrick's Cathedral, disrupts the service, and spits out the Eucharist to increase AIDS awareness. These guys really know how to put on a good show." The man pretended to be very amused by Peter because of what he wanted to do to him.

At the bars in March the needs of interviewees didn't seem any less colorful than usual. Peter was approached by a man who wanted to be treated like a lady even though he had hair on every inch of his body. Another man wanted Peter to come home and act like a lady. Once again thought Peter, two ships, one hairy, the other not, had passed in the night. He met a man who described himself as an oral expert, several tit lovers, an Italian tough guy, a muscle pig, a submissive jock, and a bevy of Long Island show queens. They came looking for the golden man of their dreams and left doubting the virtue and veracity of their own government. Peter told them they were all in the middle of a giant AIDS crematorium and they couldn't even see the fire around them. Couldn't they taste the smoke and ashes? They asked themselves whether this guy was making it all up. It would have been so much easier to believe what he was saying if he would just come home and talk about it some more in bed.

The big topics of conversation at the bars that month were *Rent* and *Birdcage*. Peter had seen both and he dismayed nearly everyone with his opinions. He said that *Rent* was the *Hair* for the AIDS Empire. He called it the first AIDS minstrel show and said that

Broadway was turning into the karaoke room for AIDS propaganda. About *Birdcage*, all he would say is that he hoped that everyone involved was taking the miracle drug, AZT.

It would be difficult to overstate the sense of urgency that Peter's troublesome presence on the gay scene engendered in the AIDS activist community. Members were staked out in bars all over the city to try and spot him. Once he was located, two of the least conspicuous AIDS activists were assigned to tail Peter and report on his every move as he made his round of the bars each night. His itinerary was unpredictable and difficult to follow. Once he was located each evening, activists from all over the city poured into the adjacent neighborhood and postered every available inch with AIDS propaganda intended to counter the effect of Peter.

Hidden cameras were used to identify the people who talked to Peter. Many of these people were later approached by AIDS activists who debriefed the men and tried to repair any damage that Peter had done to the Empire's official story.

Pictures were taken of Peter covertly and soon AIDS activists all had mug shots in their wallets. One enterprising artist who was an AIDS activist did a sketch of what he thought Peter would look like in the nude and also distributed it around town. The activists gasped when they saw his face because even the dark and tacky photos could not destroy the impression that this was a once-in-a-lifetime specimen of a man. The AIDS activists tried to keep their personal responses in check because something much larger than sex was at stake here. Peter was declared the biggest public relations threat to AIDS in New York. To have an enemy who looked like Adonis was destabilizing to many of the AIDS activists (the ones who really were gay) with libidos in working order.

A high-level AIDS activist task force was formed to do damage control on Peter. Careful gay bar intelligence had determined that Peter was spreading the word around the bars that the HIV test was a totally unreliable piece of garbage that threatened every American's health and liberty. The AIDS activists didn't like the sound of that.

Before long, thanks to a carefully constructed network of media contacts, page one stories began appearing in all the major papers in town about how the HIV test was the most accurate medical test in history. The test made lackluster lives more meaningful. A positive result could get you into venues you never dreamed of. Everyone should take the test early and often so they could avail themselves of the groundbreaking, untested drugs that the AIDS activists had forced the FDA to foist upon AIDS patients. The HIV test was a privileged rite of passage into the AIDS Empire.

One moment of hope occurred for Peter that month when he saw a story in the *Messenger* about a Tennessee woman who was suing a medical center for passing on false information that she was HIV-positive. The courts were not using her real name (neither is the virus, thought Peter), but referred to her as Jane Doe. It was just another indication of how scientifically unreliable and politically dangerous the HIV test was.

Peter had his first physical confrontation with an AIDS activist that month. It was at a bar in Midtown late in the evening. The AIDS activist had slunk in, mingled momentarily with the crowd, and then grabbed what was left of a pile of *Messengers* and quickly exited the bar. Peter caught this out of the corner of his eye and instantly pursued the man, yelling, "Put those back, moron!" The crowd parted like the Red Sea for Peter. The customers watched through the bar's big bay window as Peter grabbed the *Messengers* just as the man was about to toss them in a trash bin.

The man launched into an old-fashioned homosexual catfight by pulling Peter's hair, a move that struck the crowd inside as sacrilegious. When Peter went to pull the man's hair, he discovered to his horror that the man's hair was mobile. When the AIDS activist's toupee hit the street Peter gasped as it revealed a tattoo on his bald head that read "HIV POSITIVE." For Christ's sake, he thought, these people are stranger than anything on *The X-Files*.

The Bald AIDS Activist came unglued and started moving like a whirling dervish. All of his activist emotions were out of control and going in every direction at once. At the top of his lungs he started shouting just about every AIDS activist slogan that had ever been invented, perhaps hoping to rouse the crowd to that legendary in-your-face AIDS activism that the Empire was famous for. But maybe because his voice resembled Margaret Hamilton's in *The Wizard of Oz*, the men in the bar were howling. Some of them were doubled over in laughter and spitting out their drinks. For Peter, it was awesome to see gay men laughing at an AIDS activist. It was downright inspiring.

The activist screamed, "DRUGS INTO BODIES! DRUGS INTO BODIES! FREE AZT! FREE AZT! FASTER DRUGS! BIGGER STUDIES! TEST US NOW! TEST US NOW! AIDS CZAR OR BUST! AIDS CZAR OR BUST!" As the man got louder and louder, the laughter in the bar drowned him out.

This had never happened to an AIDS activist before. It reminded Peter of images he had seen of what had transpired after the Second World War in France—images of women who had been Nazi collaborators as they had their heads shaved and were forced to run naked through the streets while the crowds brutally beat them. Peter had a terrible premonition that history was about to take a similar horrific turn, but the matter of who would end up naked and bloody in the streets was up in the air. Maybe someday a historian might date this very moment as the beginning of America's second Civil War.

When Peter walked back into the bar, he was treated like a hero. What man doesn't stir erotically in the core of his polymorphous soul when a handsome prince triumphs over a bald gargoyle with a tacky tattoo on his head?

The man on the posters continued robbing gay bars all over Manhattan during March. Peter spent so many nights in the gay bars that he expected eventually to run into the man. If he did, he planned to ask the man what the gay bar-robbing community thought about AIDS. Had they been taken in too? Although Peter never made the acquaintance of the robber, he did make his first real New York friend that month—an old man whom Peter seemed to see at every bar around town. It was uncanny. For a while, he thought that it was not the same man, that he was actually seeing different versions of The Old Gay Clone, that maybe after a certain age all gay men start to look alike. The man had one of those faces full of crags from decades of cigarette smoke, his own and others. He looked like a gay face on Mt. Rushmore. It was a cross between an old Lillian Hellman and an old W. H. Auden.

Unlike everyone else in the bar, the man never approached

Peter. Consequently, Peter wondered if the man were blind or infirm. Given the ways of the gay kingdom, it was not surprising that Peter was intrigued by the one man who was not interested in him. One evening in a bar on the Upper West Side, Peter saw that the seat at the bar next to the old man was empty, so he sat down and started a conversation.

The man acted only slightly surprised when Peter began talking to him. The rest of the bar was in a state of shock. So this was Peter's secret. He robbed the grave. Peter must spend every evening jumping from bed to bed in nursing homes.

"Well, you've got quite a face there, kid," the old man said.

"Thank you, sir," said Peter politely.

"Sam, just Sam."

"Thank you, Sam. I bet you've seen a lot of this city, haven't you, Sam."

"What's your name, kid?"

"Peter."

"Figures."

"Tell me about New York, Sam."

"I came over in the gay section of the Mayflower. It was all downhill from there."

Sam was the kind of person who sat in the last row of a theater all his life just dying for a cigarette. You could have put Sam in a barrel of scotch and it would have aged overnight. He only seemed to have enough energy to keep a glass and a cigarette rising to his lips in tandem all night.

Sam was the most resigned gay man that Peter had ever met. Sam didn't ask a lot of questions because he had been around the gay block. He was long in the gay tooth. He had taken the gay knocks. Life had worked his last gay nerve. He knew where all the gay bodies were buried. He had burned his gay candle at both ends. His gay cup had runneth over and now the gay cup was more than half-empty.

Sam seemed to have absorbed centuries of gay experience. He had all the gay scars from all the gay wounds. If Sam, as they say, had slept with everyone that his partners had slept with, Sam had been in bed with Michelangelo, Alexander the Great, and a couple of popes. Sam's philosophy of life was the result of simmering everything he had experienced into the rich reduction of a very

gay sauce. It could be summed up simply.
Nothing ever works out.
Don't expect much.
The bad guys always win.
The worst is yet to come.
Don't bite off more than you can chew. If possible, don't bite off anything.
Keep a piece of paper in your wallet with a list of all the happy hours in town.

What the world had taken away from Sam, he seemed to be taking back in scotch and cigarettes. The bags under Sam's eyes had matching luggage everywhere on his person. Sam didn't have the best gay luck in the world. On a plane headed for the coast in the Forties, he'd had a fight with Bette Davis.

To Peter, Sam's defeatism was a force of nature. Peter took Sam's negativity as a challenge. The young, beautiful, eternal optimist would convert this wise, old, pessimistic, gay *bete noir*. Sam was truly the other side of Peter's coin. It would be a victory just to make Sam smile. A laugh would be the Resurrection.

Peter loved to hear Sam's stories. For Peter, Sam was the Old Gay Historian. He even predated Miss Thing. He was Father Thing. He didn't age because now he seemed to be as gay and as old as he could get. Peter liked the fact that Sam didn't settle for looking old and wise and sad with the other gay geezers in Manhattan's wrinkle room bar. No, Sam was still part of the scene. He chose to look old and wise and sad in bars all over town. Sam sat staring into gay space with his serial scotches, chain-smoking the night away. He took things as they came. When he coughed his smoker's cough, the foundation of the bar shook. Peter thought that Sam's lungs were like the gay caves of Pompeii. They contained the gay and lesbian first and secondhand smoke damage from the exotic closeted bars of the Thirties and Forties and Fifties. Sam's cavernous cigarette cough was the cough of the gay ages.

Of course, Sam was treated at the bars as if he were a statue that had escaped from Madame Tussaud's Waxworks. People were drawn to him as much as to Peter but by another law of gravity, the one that says that people instinctively want to lift the sheet and take a look at the body. Gay men from all generations came over to look closely at Sam at one time or another because it was like taking a peek into their own caskets. One day, if they were lucky, they would all look and be like Sam. What was that going to feel like? Was it bearable? What was the alternative?

Before long Sam and Peter became one of the most underestimated of gay entities: bar buddies. They would never sleep together, party together, have puppies together, or even eat a meal together. But this was not a connection or a commitment to be underestimated, for they were now joined at the drink. From now on, they would be a kind of couple that cared little about recognition in any State of the Union. Oh, how this sight broke the heart of *tout* New York.

If you had to pick a part of town for an assassin to live, Hell's Kitchen would be on your short list, and it was there that Peter found a studio apartment for $700 a month. The apartment was within walking distance of Angel's Bistro. When he had first called up about the apartment, he was told he could see it, but that he would be put on a list. However, when the lesbian super of the building took one look at Peter, the list evaporated. Peter was a one-man gentrification program. For some reason, lesbian supers and hot gay men are nearly always spiritual twins. Don't ask.

Peter decorated his apartment in what could be called assassin minimalism or early graduate student. He futoned the place, built unstable brick bookcases and bought a couple of inexpensive folding chairs that would never get much use. On his walks home from the Bistro he always bought a new plant until the studio looked like a lush botanical garden. The golden boy had a green thumb.

On the wall facing his bed he taped articles from the *New York Messenger*. He put up photos of scientists who had tried to expose the government's lies about the epidemic. He also hung a photo of the man who had written a book exposing many of the AIDS medications as biomedical genocide. He also put up some of the AIDS Empire posters that had been used to put the gay kingdom into its trance. Every morning when he woke up he stared at the wall. It was a constant reminder that he had come to New York for one reason and one reason only.

April

Sam was one of the great listeners in the world. Sam mulled things over. He was born to mull. Nothing seemed to surprise or faze him. He had heard it all. If he hadn't done it himself, he knew someone who had. Peter shared with Sam all his thoughts about gay men and the Empire. Over and over he told Sam in great detail that what the government was telling the public about AIDS was totally untrue.

"I'm not surprised, " was Sam's response.

"And all these gay men are just following these medical Pied Pipers over the cliff to their deaths."

"What did you expect?"

"They're all taking a test for a virus that doesn't cause the disease and then they're voluntarily taking the drugs that will kill them."

"That's the way it goes," said Sam, sadly.

"But Sam, we have to stop it. We have to wake them up."

"You can lead the gay horses to water, but you can't make them drink."

"And the *Messenger* keeps trying to save them from this fate, while they all keep trying to destroy the *Messenger*."

"There's only so much you can do, kid."

Peter asked Sam to describe gay life in the Thirties for him.

"It was rough, kid."

Then he asked him what it was like in the Forties.

"It wasn't easy."

"I bet it wasn't easy in the Fifties and the Sixties either, Sam."

"That's right, kid."

"And the Seventies, were they a killer?"

"No. The Seventies were okay."

When Sam told Peter that he had seen a movie about AIDS called *It's My Party*, Peter asked him what he thought of it.

"It was very sad," said Sam.

41

"What was the moral of the movie?"

"Take one day at a time."

Sam seemed to have seen every movie that had ever been made. He had even been an extra in some that were made in the Forties. Whenever there was a call for a depressed-man-at-a-bar type, Sam got the part. He had a great memory for the names of actors, actresses, and bit players. The only odd thing was that to Sam, the moral of every movie seemed to be, "Take one day at a time."

Peter trusted Sam so much that he told him about his plans to assassinate the AIDS epidemic.

"Couldn't you just write a show, kid?"

April brought author Leslie Feinberg to the Different Light Bookstore to sign her new book, *Transgender Warrior: Making History from Joan of Arc to RuPaul*. At the Gay and Lesbian Community Center, author Eric Rofes led a workshop based on his book, *Reinventing the Tribe: Regenerating Gay Men's Sexuality and Culture in the Ongoing Epidemic*. Since Peter was neither declaring transgender war, nor regenerating a sexuality that did not yet exist, he confined his reading to a book that he had seen one evening in the window of Coliseum Books on 57th Street. He had read about *Osler's Web* in the *Messenger*. He rushed home and read the book until he passed out at dawn.

The book seemed to confirm everything he had been reading in the *Messenger*. The author showed in 700 pages how the government was concealing a huge epidemic of AIDS in the general population by calling it Chronic Fatigue Syndrome. Not only were government scientists giving it a ridiculous name, they were saying that it was not contagious and that very few people had it, even though it was clear that its victims numbered in the millions.

Peter wanted to take the book to the gay bars and hold public readings.

It was uncanny how every symptom that was found in AIDS could also be found in people with Chronic Fatigue Syndrome, or as it was laughably called, The Yuppie Flu. (Peter wondered whether Death could be called the Yuppie Leave of Absence.) And yet from every scientific pulpit the government continued to push the line that AIDS was caused by the world's only gay retrovirus. Could no one see through this?

As he read more of *Osler's Web*, it was obvious that every scientist who spoke out and said that Chronic Fatigue Syndrome was a contagious, serious illness with links to AIDS, was quickly silenced, defamed, and defunded.

It seemed like no coincidence to Peter that every scientist who said that HIV could not be the cause of AIDS had met with a similar fate. Or worse. Faced with the omnipotence of the AIDS Empire, many dissenting voices voluntarily left the battlefield.

It was too bad that both groups of skeptical scientists could not get together, because it seemed like they had one big juicy truth between them. And they were both being silenced for the same reason. Peter suspected that the public would go ballistic if they knew what was really going on with AIDS and the Yuppie Flu. It wasn't just that heads would roll. Parts of the AIDS Empire would be burned to the ground.

One night at a bar Peter said, "Sam, it's obvious that the government doesn't want the public to know that AIDS and the Chronic Fatigue Syndrome epidemic are part of the same thing."

"Don't push the envelope, kid."

"These folks have hidden the real AIDS epidemic from the public and tricked the gay community into thinking that it's only their problem. They're the ones taking the heat for this shit."

"It was ever thus, kid."

"And they've got all these people thinking they've got the Yuppie Flu from riding in too many BMWs. They wouldn't dare try to pump yuppies with AZT. The Yuppies would tear apart the Centers for Disease Control. No, scare the bejesus out of the fags and they'll take anything you offer them. They'll beg for it."

"The beat goes on, Peter."

While Peter finished *Osler's Web* that month, the Michigan State Senate was passing a bill denying medical benefits to domestic partners at state universities. (The expression "domestic partners" made Peter think of maids or butlers who were married to each other.) An anti-violence organization came out with an annual report that in the United States, 40 gay men and lesbians had been murdered in hate crimes during the prior year. Georgia, the home of the Centers for Disease Control, which was working so hard for the medical welfare of gay folks, became the fourth state to ban gay marriages. (Peter suspected that they would grant a dispensation to people who were HIV-positive.) The rock publication *Spin Magazine* published an article accusing the government of concealing cases of AIDS in which no HIV could be found. A list management firm announced that it now had a list of 500,000 gay and lesbian names available for rental. In Washington D.C., there was a great deal of gay fur flying because the people who organized the Lesbian and Gay Freedom Festival wanted to rename their annual event "A Celebration of Lesbian, Gay, Bisexual, and Transgender People." Peter mused that, by the time you finished saying the names of gay events, they were over.

The Bald AIDS Activist with the HIV tattoo atop his head demanded that something be done. It had taken many days of Valium and therapy from a team of AIDS activist counselors to get him to stop involuntarily emitting angry AIDS activist chants. When he finally started speaking like a human being again, he pleaded with them to take control of the situation. "He's just a gay cockroach. Treat him as such!" the bald man cried.

The AIDS activists went on red alert city wide. They upped the AIDS ante. Soon toilet tissue appeared in bathrooms all over town with "Wipe AIDS off the face of the earth" printed on each panel. Colorful posters began appearing in laundry rooms that said, "While you're washing your clothes, someone with AIDS is dying." The activists had wanted to put an electronic sign up in every gay bar that, like the one for the national debt, constantly flashed the latest count of people who had died of AIDS. In light of the emergency, they wanted this sign to replace all the television sets in the bars. But this was considered a bit much even by the bar owners, who were used to kowtowing to the AIDS activists.

In order to inspire the activists to greater heights of activism, the Bald AIDS Activist had his forehead and buttocks tattooed "HIV POSITIVE." The activists arranged for the mayor to give the man the key to the city for his dedication to HIV activism. The activists hoped that Peter saw the ceremony on television. The activists had worked very hard to get City Hall to support their agenda. They even succeeded in getting the mayor to refer to the activist as "girlfriend" when he made the commendation. This new wave of activism proved to be as effective as the Bay of Pigs invasion. An activist poll of two gay bars in the Village showed that half the gay men were familiar with a hot young man who was going around saying that where AIDS was concerned, they had all been sold a bill of goods.

Exasperation was growing at a rapid clip in the AIDS activist community. Peter was the biggest challenge they had seen since the *Messenger* began publishing articles exposing fraud in AZT research. In that case they had stepped up their propaganda campaign to such an extent that several of the AIDS activists had been hospitalized for chanting exhaustion. But they had succeeded. Thousands of gay men had taken AZT despite the *Messenger's* warnings. Thousands of *dead* gay men. But the *Messenger* was not a twenty-three-year-old with a surfer's body and a drop dead gorgeous face. This very difficult case was going to call for a more persuasive approach. One of the AIDS activists who had just gotten back from a series of gay sensitivity training sessions at the National Institutes of Health was the first to put the idea on the table.

"We'd better send for the Avuncular Gay Physician."

"Oh, no, not the Avuncular Gay Physician!" several of the activists shrieked.

The activist in charge of AIDS aromatherapy said "Don't you think we should save him in case we get desperate?"

"But we are desperate. If we don't move quickly, the whole gay community will be infected with that kid's ideas."

And so, with great trepidation, a select delegation of AIDS activist leaders requested a closed door meeting with the Avuncular Gay Physician.

There hadn't been such a power gathering since the Berkeley Surprise when one of the nation's leading retrovirologists announced that there was no way that HIV could be the cause of AIDS. That had been a very close call, but it had been handled deftly by the Avuncular Gay Physician's iron fist. He knew the meaning of a surgical strike. The Mafia had its Don of Dons. To the leaders who were headed to the AGP's penthouse, he was the Doctor of Doctors. Whenever gay or lesbian doctors across the country had a problem of scientific, political, or traffic ticket nature they called the Avuncular Gay Physician. Many a person was convinced that he had direct lines to the White House, Congress, the National Institutes of Health and Carol Channing.

The leaders of all the most important divisions of AIDS activism were there. Immunology, Virology, Vaccinology, Neurology, Condomology, Behavior Modification, Propaganda, and Bar-Disco Relations. They all arrived in separate rented cars accompanied by plainclothes AIDS activists.

There was an ominous, hushed tone in the rich surroundings of the penthouse as one by one they paid their respects to the Doctor of Doctors. For many of these activists, this was their first taste of great American power and wealth. They moved into a large room paneled with dark wood and they all sat at a large round table beneath a massive chandelier. The light was low and the shadows of crises fell across their faces.

"Let us begin," the Avuncular Gay Physician said ceremoniously.

Immunology spoke first.

"Doctor of Doctors, this Goldilocks is threatening the whole AIDS empire. He's full of tricks. We must not underestimate him."

"He wouldn't be getting all of this attention if he weren't so cute," said Virology.

"Thanks to him all kinds of silly queens have been going to their dictionaries and looking up the word 'genocide,'" said Condomology.

"If people start thinking that something's wrong with the HIV test, our whole international agenda could be set back decades," cried Behavior Modification.

Propaganda asked that the lights be turned off so that the Avuncular Gay Physician could see the slides.

"Turn on the projector and lets see the first slide."

"That's him talking to a gay fireman, Doctor."

"Next," said the doctor.

"There he is with a pedicurist." They were deep in conversation and the pedicurist was staring at Peter's feet.

"Next."

"That's him talking to an aide to a city councilwoman. Look at how intensely the man is studying Peter, Doctor."

"Good God! Next."

The next slide showed Peter at Splash talking to a man in a clown costume.

"Who is that gay clown?" asked the Avuncular Gay Physician.

"A man from Jersey. You can see how this could spread, Doctor. Every clown in New Jersey has probably heard Peter's story."

Bar-Disco Relations stood up and hit his fist on the table. "It's that goddamned mug of his. If he looked like Ed Asner, we wouldn't be sitting here in this situation."

"But we are, Blanche, we are," said the Doctor.

Some of the AIDS activists were so overcome by the Doctor's wit that they fell out of their chairs laughing.

"Well, he doesn't have to continue looking that good," said Neurology, ominously.

"Now, now, we won't let it come to that. Is there another slide?"

"Doctor, this is Peter talking to a hustler."

"That's very unfortunate," said the Doctor. "They get around and some of them are our best patients. They're always so grateful. And they pay in cash. Turn the lights back on please."

The Avuncular Gay Physician sat back in his chair and thought deeply. "So what is it exactly that he is saying to the educatees?" "Educatees" is the term that AIDS activists used for gay men who were not yet AIDS activists.

All the leaders looked at each other nervously until Virology spoke up.

"I'm glad you're sitting down, Doctor of Doctors. He is telling people that everything the government and the AIDS activists are telling the public is a lie. He is saying that the only difference between the government and the AIDS activists is that the government dresses better. He tells them that all the top AIDS researchers are crooks and that the people under them are cowardly morons. Every night he uses a different word for the HIV test. Sometimes he calls it garbage. Other times, he uses words like hoax, baloney, crock, and bullshit. He tells some people that they should launch a class action lawsuit against the government for lying about the epidemic. He tells people that if they're being given toxic treatments by their doctors, they should walk out of the practice and not forget to tell the doctor that he is performing unethical medical experiments. And worst of all, Doctor . . . he encourages people to use their imaginations to sabotage the AIDS activists in any way they can."

Everyone in the room was visibly shaken.

"Where did this little whippersnapper come from?"

"He materialized in New York City some time after Christmas. He tells people that he came from out west. He's only an English Major."

"An English Major?" said the doctor. "An English Major. No wonder. This is what happens when those people find that they can't get good jobs. Does he get his information from where I think he gets it?"

"Yes, Doctor of Doctors. From the *New York Messenger*."

"Damn the *Messenger*," said the doctor.

As if it was a cue to begin a chant, all of the leaders began to shout in unison.

"DAMN THE *MESSENGER*! DAMN THE *MESSENGER*! DAMN THE *MESSENGER*!"

"Okay boys, calm down. When I'm done with that son of a bitch, he'll have AIDS awareness up the wazoo. I'll give him some medical advice he can't refuse."

One of the AIDS activists fell to his knees and kissed the AGP's hand. With great relief in his voice he said, "Thank you, thank you, Doctor of Doctors."

Early one evening (in bar time) the following week, a limousine pulled up to Rome in Chelsea where Peter was being courted by an Irish Tenor from the Gay, Lesbian, Bisexual and Transgender Chorus. Two rather tough but Armani-clad men got out and walked into the bar and asked to have a private word with Peter. In a corner of the bar they told him that the most powerful gay doctor in America requested that he join him for dinner the following week at Montrachet, one of the city's best French restaurants. They explained to Peter that the Avuncular Gay Physician would be speaking to Peter on behalf of all the gay and lesbian doctors in America.

The invitation made Peter a little edgy, but the challenge of dealing with the whole gay medical establishment in one fell swoop excited him. He agreed to have dinner with the Avuncular Gay Physician. They told him to be sure to wear a jacket and tie.

At Montrachet the following week, the Avuncular Gay Physician was royally polite to Peter. They were seated at the best table and the AGP immediately ordered the most expensive wine in the house.

"Well, Peter, you're really making a name for yourself in town, and you've only been here for....?"

"A few months."

"It takes some people years to make the impression you've made. Everyone I've talked to says that you're surprisingly intelligent."

"Thank you, sir."

"And everyone is very impressed that you've learned so much about AIDS. You've clearly done a lot of reading on the subject. That's admirable, in a way."

"Thank you."

"But of course, you know the difference between doing a little reading and being a board certified physician."

"Yes, sir...boy, do I."

"Well, let's order. Please have anything you want."

Peter made a point of ordering the least expensive item on the menu, which annoyed the AGP. He wanted Peter to be eating the most expensive item when he lowered the boom. This little prick was cramping his style.

"Are you sure you don't want the lobster? Everyone says that it's fabulous here."

"Thank you, but the chicken looks fabulous enough."

Peter also barely drank the wine. He lifted the glass and let it touch his lips, but he wanted his head to be clear as a pistol.

As he looked around the restaurant, he thought about how wonderful and romantic a place it would be to bring a lover—if a certain government were not lying about a certain epidemic.

Peter tried to keep looking, pleasantly but defiantly, into the doctor's eyes, which were trained upon him. This had a devastating effect on the doctor, because even though he was avuncular,

49

Peter was a looker and the doctor was only human. And even though the AGP had trained in psychological warfare at Langley, Peter's stare was lethal. He was a human laser.

The AGP started to sweat and mopped his furrowed brow with his handkerchief.

"Is it getting hot in here or is it me?"

"I feel quite comfortable."

The doctor felt like his temperature was soaring, as if he were getting the flu or meningitis. This manipulative little bastard, he thought. He wasn't quite prepared for the psychic invulnerability that was sitting across the table from him.

"Peter, let me tell you about the history of gay people and medicine."

As the appetizers arrived, he began with Hippocrates and the drag queens of Athens and in painful detail he brought the story all the way up to AIDS. He left nothing out. He even paused in the Middle Ages to tell a little joke about enemas and the lesbian nuns of Avignon.

"You're really well-educated," Peter said, trying to hide his irritation with the pedantry.

"Thank you," the AGP said. "Harvard, Yale, Actor's Studio."

"You certainly are more cultivated than most of the gay doctors I've met."

"Oh I know what you mean. Some of them are, shall we say, mountain people?"

"Oh, we shall," said Peter.

"But they are our brothers and sisters, we mustn't forget."

"No," said Peter, "and we mustn't forget that our patients are our brothers and sisters."

"No, of course not," said the doctor, "Power to the people!"

For a split second, Peter's eyes crossed.

"Now, Peter, I hope you don't mind if I get a little serious."

"No...not at all, Doctor."

"Do you know what gay doctors were before AIDS?"

"No...what?'

"Clap doctors. That's all we were. Penis pinchers. Swab takers. That's all we were. Do you know what that's like? Do you realize what that's like?"

"No."

50

"We had the best upbringing. We attended the most expensive schools. We had the deepest tans. We had front row seats at the opera, and still we were only clap doctors. Do you know what other doctors would do behind our backs when we showed up at the major teaching hospitals in New York? Do you know what sound they made as we walked down the hallway?"

"They didn't."

"Yes, they did. They clapped. It was their little joke about the gay doctors. They clapped behind our backs. And do you know how they treated the gay patients?"

"I can imagine."

"In their minds, they were all clap patients. No matter what was wrong with them, they were clap cases. Even the lesbians. That's how your people were treated. Until . . ."

"Until?"

"Until AIDS. AIDS changed everything. AIDS was Rosa Parks refusing to sit on the back of the bus. After AIDS, we gay doctors were someone. AIDS got us across the River Jordan. And all our patients became special patients. Suddenly we were invited to the National Institutes of Health and the Centers for Disease Control. Imagine that! All us little clap doctors. Being appointed to committees in Washington and Atlanta. Did you know that the head of the N.I.H. once looked respectfully in my eyes and asked me to pass the salt? And all our patients suddenly became the most pampered patients in all kinds of special programs with the best new experimental treatments that this country has to offer. Now we're on every medical panel and board in America. Data on our patients constantly flows to Washington. And we're courted by every major pharmaceutical company listed on the American Stock Exchange. Do you know how many times these companies have taken me to the Caribbean? I can't count them. Me, the little clap doctor from Harvard. Look at me, Peter, I'm your Rosa Parks!"

The doctor's face was beet-red and the sweat was flying out in all directions, but he continued.

"Don't get in the way of gay progress, Peter. Don't make us all clap patients and clap doctors again. Don't send Rosa to the back of the bus again."

"I'll do my best," said Peter, a little mystified.

Dessert came, but the Doctor continued to look disturbingly red. Everyone in the restaurant was now aware of his bizarre coloration. He had been getting a little loud and Peter was somewhat embarrassed.

"Peter, what if you're wrong about AIDS? You're not a doctor. You're not a scientist. 100,000 doctors disagree with you. Have you thought about the consequences of being wrong?"

"Doctor, what if you're wrong? What are the consequences? Have you thought about that?"

"Peter, I hardly know you, but I feel like a father towards you. I'm concerned about you. I'm worried about your mental well-being. Maybe the epidemic has gotten to you. Maybe the stress of being all alone in your opinions is distorting your judgment. Maybe I can help. Maybe I can get you psychological help."

"Don't patronize me, you toxic old fruitcake."

The doctor paused and then tried to say something.

"Mffttopod mftof pod," he said.

"What?"

"Mffftopodmftpod," the doctor said, his face getting redder.

Then the doctor slumped to the side and fell to the floor. There was very little movement except for one eye that kept blinking. At first people thought he might have choked on something but Peter told the waiters and manager that he hadn't eaten anything for a few minutes. The ambulance was there in five minutes and the AGP was in the emergency room in another fifteen. The young man who had come to New York to assassinate the AIDS epidemic had given the Doctor of Doctors, the Avuncular Gay Physician, a stroke.

May

Self-appointment was one of the best fringe benefits in the gay world. It began in the act of coming out. Declaring oneself to be openly gay was the first act of self-appointment. But in so many cases it didn't stop there. Shortly after coming out, many people declared themselves to be gay poets, gay novelists, gay philosophers, gay journalists and gay politicians. This may be the reason that the literature of the gay world is of Nobel caliber and it may explain why gay politics are revered and feared wherever people cast ballots and in several places where they don't. Self-appointed people grew into self-appointed committees and self-appointed committees were forever announcing that they were self-appointed movements.

If you hated gay people and you were hanging out in some rabid antigay compound of a cult in the West or Midwest, you could get on a plane on a Friday and by Monday you could be a self-appointed gay in New York, making the rounds in the gay bars, gyms and social organizations. What was involved in being gay anyway? You just had to say you were gay. The gay world was a great place to be yourself or not yourself. No one carded you. There were no road checks or identification papers. You could even speak for all the gays if you yourself weren't really gay. There were no labels telling the buyer to beware. If Alice had been a lesbian, in the world of gay self-appointment she would have found her Wonderland.

Needless to say, in the late Eighties and early Nineties, the most active area of self-appointment was within the AIDS Empire. The range of characters who had appointed themselves AIDS spokesactivists was stunning. The list included former stockbrokers, military personnel, art dealers, professional bowlers, card sharks, doormen and most unexpectedly of all, gay mimes. At the blessed moment of self-appointment, the names of all AIDS spokesactivists were automatically entered on the Rolodexes of all the top AIDS reporters in the city. If a reporter needed a pithy quote from a credible source to go into a hard-hitting AIDS article, he would just speed-dial one of the self-appointed AIDS spokesactivists. Thus were the lives of the city's one million gay and lesbian citizens represented and spoken for without a single one of them having to pick up a telephone.

If you happened to be a self-appointed AIDS intellectual in May, you could have attended a colloquium at the Center for Lesbian and Gay Studies called "AIDS, Race, and the Shift from Acting Up to Assimilation." In the endless game of new off-putting names for things gay, Peter expected that the Center would one day be known as the Center for AIDS Studies. Not since Hegel had discovered thesis, antithesis, synthesis, and prosthesis had such a powerful intellectual organizing principle as AIDS been discovered. The AIDS Empire was fertile ground for self-appointed gay intellectuals. Everything was happening so fast. From lesbian postmodernism to transsexual deconstruction, all roads led inexorably in one direction: AIDS.

Another event that many self-appointed AIDS intellectuals found themselves attending that month was held at the Gay and Lesbian Center on the 8th. For two hours, one could learn how to make a living will for one's own medical self-determination, so that after one had taken all the miracle treatments for AIDS, one's lover could take one off of one's life support machinery. If one so chose. The discussion of such intimate rituals had been integrated into the gestalt of gay romance like the heart-shaped bathtubs of the Poconos.

In May, the days grew longer, the sunshine that filled the bedrooms of the city in the morning seemed honeyed, the first flowers of Central Park peeked out of their winter closets, and of course a young gay man's fancy turned to the AIDS Walk. To Peter, the AIDS Walk, which was supposed to raise money for AIDS research, ranked near the top of events that caught the absurd essence of the Empire. For years the Walk had been growing and growing, but it was like Moses leading his people in circles. They walked and they walked. They raised money and they raised more money. But all the money ended up in the hands of the same government-approved researchers with the same government-approved ideas. A lot of the money had actually ended up killing people. But none of the walkers had any idea this was happening. They were all so earnest and cheerful and caring and they tried to walk and walk the plague away.

As the AIDS walkers circled Central Park endlessly, a Florida man who had strangled a gay man to death used as his defense that the gay man had AIDS and wanted to die. The alleged strangler's lawyers told the *Palm Beach Post* that "We will show that the victim was a sophisticated and intelligent terminally ill patient who had a lurid death fantasy and sought out a gullible young man to facilitate that wish." (Well, maybe that explains the whole AIDS epidemic, thought Peter.)

No event carried as much potential fallout for AIDS that month as the publication of an exposé by the *Wall Street Journal*. The May first article revealed that top officials of the Centers for Disease Control admitted that they had lied to the public about AIDS for over a decade. The report suggested that the government had exaggerated the risk of AIDS to the general population. The CDC had bombarded the country with the message that anyone could get AIDS while privately knowing the opposite. Or so they now said. They were admitting that they kept two sets of books on the epidemic. How do we know that they're not keeping three or four, wondered Peter.

The *Wall Street Journal* reported that the CDC was pulling back from its everyone-gets-AIDS message because money for so-called AIDS prevention was not going to the groups that the CDC had really targeted. Heterosexuals were not supposed to be getting in on the AIDS goodies.

It is always a reassuring moment in history when a government institution admits it is lying. In Peter's mind, what was even more reassuring was the complexity of the CDC's lie because even at the moment of truth-telling, there was yet another lie peeking out of the revelation itself.

By saying that heterosexuals were not really at risk for AIDS, the CDC was neatly concealing the fact that millions of heterosexuals were already trapped in their own wildfire of a plague, namely, the Yuppie Flu. Chronic Fatigue Syndrome. Epstein Barr disease. Little AIDS. AIDS lite. AIDS minor. Covert AIDS. Call it what you want to take people's attention off the reality of it, but the unmistakable rat eyes of AIDS could be seen lurking inside the secret medical disaster.

What a clever government, thought Peter.

The CDC's willingness to lie about the two faces of the same epidemic had an interesting collateral effect. By causing the nation to latex-up, from surgical gloves to condoms, it had sentenced thousands of Americans to the crippling and life-threatening latex allergies that they were developing all over the country. Just kidding about AIDS, folks. Sorry you're now in a wheel chair hooked up to an oxygen tank.

The *Wall Street Journal* reported that the CDC had hired a public relations firm to help them package the lie they told the public. Within a couple of years, the country, according to most polls, was successfully duped.

Peter wondered whether a PR firm had come up with the idea of admitting that they lied about AIDS in order to lie anew to the public about the connection between AIDS and the Yuppie Flu. While some scientists estimated that there were four million cases of this sister form of AIDS, the CDC, when not arguing that Chronic Fatigue Syndrome did not really even exist, admitted to only 10,000 cases, if in fact it did exist. Go figure.

Peter wanted to stop strangers on the street and ask them why they believed anything that the CDC said. But if anybody had asked him what the CDC was, he would have been depressed, so he didn't.

Peter thought it was ironic that in the same month the National Lesbian and Gay Journalists Association announced an annual prize of $2,500 for recognizing excellence in print journalism on issues related to the gay and lesbian community. Peter knew that it would never go to a gay or lesbian journalist who exposed the fact that the government was lying to every single gay and lesbian citizen in the country about AIDS because not a single gay or lesbian journalist, except the ones in the *New York Messenger*, had bothered to even consider the possibility. *Au contraire.* One member of the National Lesbian and Gay Journalists Association told Peter that he suspected that every member of the association hated the *New York Messenger*.

Things just got better and better at Angel's Bistro. One of the smartass food reviewers wrote that the best things to eat at the restaurant were the waiters, and floods of reservations started coming in. By waiters, of course, he meant Peter.

Angel's Bistro quickly became one of the top hangouts for models because word spread that there was a new top male model in town and he wasn't even a model. It was a bit of a turnoff for Peter because every one of the models who came in seemed to be wearing a red ribbon. The entire international modeling community seemed to have become an arm of AIDS fundraising and activism.

Peter's four-star waiting brought a lot of repeat business to the restaurant. Scores of older women seemed to be coming back to look at him as though he were being considered for roles ranging from gigolo to boy toy.

Peter did take a special interest in a very well-kept fiftyish woman who had a Garboesque face and a striking head of prematurely silver hair. She had more life in her than a twenty-year-old and she was constantly in motion at the table when she brought her friends to lunch. Somehow she knew what days Peter worked because she came in for virtually every one of his lunch shifts.

Peter was intrigued by the silver lady because every time he passed her table she seemed to be saying that something sucked. The government sucked. The president sucked. Congress sucked. The media sucked. Hollywood sucked. The theater sucked. Wall Street sucked. Peter thought that she had an interesting take on things.

The woman could barely take her eyes off Peter. The intensity of her glances made Peter nervous. She looked at him as though she had known him years ago and was trying to figure out when and where.

As Peter was laying down the check one day at the woman's table, he overheard her younger companion ask her to come to a masked AIDS charity ball.

The silver woman snapped back, "Not on your life. AIDS is a racket."

"You can say that again," chimed in Peter as he walked away from the table.

When he came back for the credit card he apologized for

57

butting in.

"Oh don't be sorry. I'm thrilled someone agrees with me. I think it's the biggest racket in history."

Peter smiled at the woman and went off with her card. Her name was Cornelia Ramsey Wade. It was an American Express Platinum card. It was not rejected.

When Peter returned to the table with the receipt, his eyes locked with those of the silver woman. Something was being turned inside out. What was going on between them was beyond the reach of their conscious minds.

A few minutes after Cornelia left the restaurant, she returned and sat down at the bar where she ordered an Irish coffee. She watched Peter and waited for an opportunity to wave him over. When the moment came, she said, "Peter—I know your name is Peter. My name is Cornelia Ramsey Wade. I must see you. I know you're gay. I'm not some old *Valley of the Dolls* hussy trying to pick you up. But any gay man who thinks that AIDS is a racket, well…listen, I just would like to talk to you. Can you meet me at the Plaza tomorrow around five for a drink?"

"I love the Plaza," Peter said. "The first floor looks like the inside of the Titanic."

Peter really did love the Plaza. He had never had a drink or a meal there, but during his walks around Central Park, he would often end up walking through the reception areas of the Plaza. It was one of those free dreamy things you could do in New York. No matter what he was wearing, he looked like he belonged there. He loved hearing violin music coming from the center of the ground floor. If New York was one big house, this was its dining room. At its tables there seemed to be seated elegant families from every wealthy generation of New York's history. The calm, self-satisfied faces of the rich were faces that never changed. And the Oak Room bar looked like its dark expensive wooden walls retained all the business secrets that undergirded the very existence of the city.

She was already sitting in the corner of the bar drinking a drink before the drink when Peter arrived. She was obviously nervous and excited. When he walked through the bar's entrance, she lit up, but then everyone who saw him enter the bar did, too.

They exchanged greetings and he sat down. For several long seconds, they just stared at each other and smiled.

Out of the blue she said, "Peter, You don't particularly care what women want, do you?"

"No," he replied. "Not really."

"I like that in a man," she said. "I have to know you."

"You do?"

"Yes, absolutely. I have to know you for a reason."

"What's the reason.'

"I don't know. But there is one. I can tell. I get vibes."

After they had ordered two vodka martinis, Peter said, "I want to know why you said that AIDS is a racket. I also want to know why you say everything in this country sucks."

"Which first?"

"Why is AIDS a racket?"

"That's easy."

"Why?"

"Can't you tell?" she asked.

"Yes," he said, "but why do *you* think that?"

"Well, for starters, they keep raising money and nothing really ever happens. They pretend it does, but nothing ever happens. I don't see it ending. And none of the reporting about AIDS makes much sense."

"I know a lot about AIDS."

"Well, there's the reason we met," she said. "I don't."

"What do you know a lot about?"

"That's a good question. Let me think....I know a lot about journalism."

"You do?"

"Yes, all my boyfriends have been reporters."

"Are you married?"

"Are you kidding? I said all my boyfriends have been reporters."

"Are you a reporter?"

"No."

"What do you do for a living?"

"I read books. I think. I brunch with the wolves."

"For a living?"

"I don't do anything for a living. I have something more important than a rent-controlled apartment. I have a little trust fund. I am the last person in the world who should have a trust fund. But then, somebody's got to keep the Plaza and Angel's Bistro afloat."

When the waiter brought the drinks, he had a look on his face like he'd seen this kind of relationship frequently in the Oak Room. He knew who would be paying for the drinks.

"Tell me more about AIDS," Cornelia said.

"If you'll tell me more about journalism."

Thus did the curious intellectual marriage between the twenty-three-year-old assassin of the AIDS epidemic and the fifty-something newspaper groupie begin. When real soulmates meet for the first time, it's like two hard drives exchanging all of their data simultaneously. In two hours, the first data transfer between the golden boy and the silver woman was thorough and exhilarating. There were no flaky abstractions about the nature of gay men distorting Cornelia's vision of Peter. Without clichés or bigoted cattiness, she could see the purity of his being.

Cornelia was a woman who had been born on the night of a full moon and all her life she had obviously given the planets a run for their money. From her strange vantage point in the cosmos, she seemed to know how much everything in America sucked as well as everything about journalism, which also sucked, because she appeared to have slept with every journalist on the East Coast except Woodward and Bernstein.

Peter was fascinated by her history. If information really was power, Cornelia had slept in the beds that ruled America. Whenever she mentioned a boyfriend, Peter saw a byline.

"In some newsrooms, I'm known as the ink-stained babe," she said. "It's all Carl and Bobby's fault."

The Sixties were Cornelia's formative years. The Watergate years were her orgasmic ones. Cornelia hated Nixon so much that Woodward and Bernstein became the very standard by which all other men were measured. Cornelia had gone from bed to bed and from newsroom to newsroom trying to recreate the erotic feelings she felt throughout the period when these two news studs screwed Nixon. There would never be a period like it, but Cornelia was driven by some deep need to make it all happen again.

"And that's how I learned the hard way that journalists suck."

"Oh."

"None of them have the balls that Carl and Bobby did. Watergate scared them all. They almost brought down the whole country. Reporters are just a bunch of pussies now. I've slept with so many of them I feel like a lesbian."

"Very interesting."

"Peter, I'll tell you one thing I learned from vamping around all these bullshit artists. This country's in deep doo-doo. We've got bad karma. Very, very bad karma."

Cornelia then outlined the entire state of the nation for Peter.

America had a terrible date with destiny. Something awful was going to happen, she could just feel it. Part of her even secretly longed for it. The worst karma in history had descended on the country that was the great hope of the world. It was everywhere. They're all gonna say it's the millennium, she told Peter, but it's the karma. It was invisible and amorphous. Something profoundly grotesque had happened to America since Watergate. Cornelia dated part of it to the restoration of the death penalty. Prisons were growing faster than sunflowers in August, she said. America was losing its mind. It was on a rampage. Karmic sickness was everywhere. Americans were tying an elaborate noose around their own necks. Reporters all over the country were karmicly challenged and afraid to report the real truth about anything because America had become a house of cards.

"Nobody knows what is happening or what they're doing. And I hold all the dickheads I've slept with since Watergate partly responsible for this mess. I can't wait to see their faces when the whole thing blows."

When Peter told her the dark unbelievable tales of the AIDS Empire, Cornelia's eyes began to look a little crazed. She felt like she was sitting across from one of the sons of Carl and Bobby. She had always suspected that something was fishy about AIDS. What Peter told her made her a little ashamed of her obsession with Vietnam and Watergate. This was so much bigger. But all the old excitement was suddenly coming back. She was watching the planes napalm the villages in Viet Nam. She was watching Sergeant Calley being tried for My Lai. She was watching Westmoreland sweat bullets on the nightly news. She was looking into Johnson's pathetic, dissembling eyes. She was witnessing the secret bombing in Cambodia. She was listening to Bob Haldeman lie to Congress. She was looking at the cops cracking heads open in Chicago. She was watching the Saturday Night Massacre. As Peter finished his story about AIDS, Cornelia could see Nixon boarding the Presidential helicopter for the last time, giving his last victory sign. AIDS was all that and more. If Peter had been a straight man, she would have rented a room upstairs and demanded that he make love to her. She was that high. All of a sudden she was an undergraduate again, skinny dipping at UCLA with flowers in her hair.

"Peter, this is sensational!"

"Sensational?"

"Why it's even groovy. It's fabulous!"

"Groovy?"

"It sounds like the whole Nixon White House just moved over to the National Institutes of Health and the Centers for Disease Control. Peter, do you realize what you're saying?"

"What?"

"You're saying that every man woman and child in America has been lied to about the most serious plague in the history of mankind."

"Well, yes, I guess."

"Don't you realize what's gonna happen when people find this stuff out?"

"What?"

"It's gonna be a total bad karma blowout. I see marches and sit-ins and teach-ins. I see universities being shut down. I see marches on Washington. This could get so wild that some of the lower I.Q. states could start seceding from the union. We could come close to civil war. The music and the sex are gonna be great. All kinds of new drugs no one has ever thought of will make their way to the streets. People will start dancing again. And the clothes! Women like me are finally going to have something to wear again. Now I can see it so clearly. The whole country's gonna go. All I can say is groovy, groovy, groovy. Let the Sixties begin! Peter, you have brought me the most wonderful gift."

"I have?"

"You've given me the gift of AIDSgate."

"AIDSgate?"

"Can't you just picture it? The cover of every paper in the country. Even the putzes I've been sleeping with won't be able to

62

keep this quiet. There will be Congressional hearings. People are gonna have to get off their rich lazy butts and start reporting again."

"Well, they haven't so far."

"But can't you see? We've met. We were meant to meet. Can't you feel it? The karma is on your side. It's beneath your wings. Listen Peter, I want you to come back to my place and let me cook you a great dinner. I want to hear every detail about this epidemic of lies. But you must promise me one thing. You must never describe the interior of my apartment to anyone."

"That's weird."

"Honey, I'm weird, and I'm just getting started."

Cornelia Ramsey Wade lived on the Upper West Side in a large two bedroom apartment in a pre-war building that had the impregnability of Fort Knox. The doorman tried not to look judgmental when they entered the building, but he couldn't help himself. Peter expected the interior to look like it had been done by Ralph Lauren, but he should have guessed Peter Max.

As Cornelia pushed the door open to her apartment, Peter felt dizzy from the Day-Glo colors that were everywhere.

"Welcome to the Sixties," she said.

It was an understatement. There wasn't a square inch in the spacious apartment that wasn't decorated with something from the Sixties. There were priceless posters advertising legendary concerts of the Sixties on every wall. The walls were Dylaned and Baezed and Joplined. There was enough Joni Mitchell imagery to satisfy the most obsessive fan. The whole apartment was punctuated by Beatleness. Cornelia was the real fifth Beatle. From certain angles, it looked like the entire British invasion had taken place in this apartment. There was an urn in the corner and Cornelia swore that it contained some of Jimi Hendrix's ashes. There were anti-war posters that American historians would have killed for. Some of them were not even known to exist. Cornelia's apartment bespoke a woman who had a feminine side, a masculine side and a Pottery Barn side

The *pièce de résistance* of the apartment was the huge couch that was upholstered with a blowup of Richard Nixon's face. The entire

63

wall behind the couch bore only the ten foot faces of two men: Woodward and Bernstein. Night and day, as she lay on Nixon's face, they stared down at Cornelia and the late president that they had bagged. She had truly turned her home into a Sixties counter-cultural castle. Peter once again had to promise he would never reveal the contents of the apartment to anyone. She said there were thousands of secret Sixties apartments like it all over the country, all of them waiting for the right moment, all waiting for a sign.

She took Peter into the living room, sat him down on Nixon's face, and told him to wait while she slipped into something more comfortable. After a few minutes, she asked him to join her in the bedroom. He gulped

If the rest of the apartment was a shrine to the Sixties and Watergate, the bedroom was its altar. How many of us sleep at night beneath the giant watchful eyes of Katherine Graham and Ben Bradlee? The rest of the room was done in early psychedelic and middle flower power. Some of the room looked like it had been moved in one piece by a crane from Haight Ashbury.

Not knowing what this was all about, Peter entered the room a little nervously. She was no longer dressed in the expensive little black cocktail dress with gold jewelry that was her signature out-fit in public. She was in something that resembled the muumuus his mother used to wear on the patio when she barbecued during the summer. It went down to her feet and it was full-length. She was also wearing a headband around her silver mane and a pair of odd looking shoes he had never seen before.

"Peter, welcome. Welcome to the Sixties."

"Thank you," said Peter.

"Peter, do you know what I'm wearing?"

"Well, not exactly."

"It's a granny dress, Peter. The real thing."

She walked over to her clothes closet and pulled both doors open. It was full of dozens of the same kind of dresses.

"Granny dresses, Peter. All of them. I'm ready."

"For what?"

"The Sixties. There's not a dress in that closet that wasn't designed by a woman who died of a drug overdose. Everything I wear is totally pure. Peter, you're gonna make it all happen again, I can just feel it. My biological clock is ticking. It has to happen before I get Alzheimer's."

"Well, I'll do my best. What are those?" he said, pointing to her feet.

"My, you really are a baby. They're Earth Shoes. Earth Shoes from Versace."

She walked over to her dresser and put on a weird looking pair of glasses.

"Peter, granny glasses. Now you know that this is serious. Now I feel more like myself. Let's eat."

She took him into a huge country kitchen which Cornelia called her Earth Mother kitchen.

"Peter, I know what I'm gonna make for you. I'm gonna make you something very special. My Carole King *Tapestry* chicken casserole. I'll put on the CD."

With Carole King singing that she felt like a natural woman, and a nice big half-gallon of chilled white wine flowing into two happy glasses, Cornelia moved around the kitchen with the speed and grace of Samantha on *Bewitched*. She told Peter that she had learned to cook when she got a job in the only meat-eating lesbian commune in California. Before he knew it, Peter was devouring the Earth Motheriest chicken casserole he had ever tasted. He was on the cusp of a friendship that felt like home. As for their conversation, wave after wave of Watergate, the Sixties and AIDSgate hit the shore of their magical evening. Both their heads were spinning with subversive ideas and camaraderie. It was too bad that she wasn't a man and twenty years younger. It was too bad that he wasn't a straight man and...and well, that he wasn't a straight man. But that was all a matter of karma which Cornelia knew better than to challenge.

As they were winding up their coffee and Peter was looking at his watch, Cornelia knew that he was going to be the kind of friend you always wanted to stay another hour no matter what time it was.

And objectively speaking, they barely knew each other.

Impulsively, she said, "I want to adopt you."

"What?" He laughed.

"I want to adopt you."

"Why?"

"Because you're the gay son I never had." They both laughed.

"Don't be silly."

"I'm serious. You're now officially adopted. You're certainly better looking than the gay sons my friends have."

"But I already have a mother."

"Now you'll have two."

"Well, it might help me get into more lesbian events if I tell them I have two mothers."

Before he finally left, she took him up to her rooftop and they went out into the cool clear evening air. Cornelia pointed to the sky and Peter thought he saw a handful of stars in the east. "Just as I thought," said Cornelia. "They're all exactly where they're supposed to be. I want you to touch the stars and move the earth."

Flowers poured in from all four corners of the AIDS Empire for the fallen Avuncular Gay Physician as he recovered slowly from his devastating stroke. All the senior retrovirologists from the National Cancer Institute sent bouquets, even those who hadn't stolen viruses from other countries. The National Organization of AIDS Hospices and Hideaways sent a ton of roses. Lesbians For a Bigger Slice of The AIDS Pie sent a crate of oranges and grapefruits. A thoughtful group of zoologists from New England sent the freeze dried body of the first monkey involved in AIDS research. Five of the nation's leading biological warfare researchers anonymously sent a large plant that had a blinking human eye in it. The biggest flower productions came from the pharmaceutical companies for which the AGP had done testing on his patients. All told, the companies that sent their respects represented several thousand colorful side effects in the bodies of his AIDS patients. The Gay, Lesbian, Bisexual and Transgender Funeral Directors Association sent 100 lilies with a small casket attached to each flower. They knew which side their bread was buttered on.

The AIDS activists showed their affection and support by posting two armed AIDS activists outside the AGP's hospital room. They didn't want to take any chances. If Peter had done this to the Doctor of Doctors, what else was he capable of?

The first overt signs of mortality in a man of the AGP's stature inevitably set off a power struggle among his potential successors in the AIDS empire. Whoever replaced him would speak to and for the gay kingdom at a crucial time when more and more of the AIDS Empire's AIDS agenda needed to be put into place. Speculation about possible heirs to the throne included the lesbian doctor who had succeeded in getting over three thousand men on AZT, and the doctor who had convinced a Wisconsin school district to make every Monday HIV Prevention Day. Some people thought it would be hard to turn down the lesbian gynecologist in California who had gotten the Women's AIDS Investment Circle to declare that any scientist who said HIV was not the cause of AIDS was a threat to American women's health. But the sentimental favorite was the Boston Doctor who examined his patients in the same leather outfit that he wore to the S&M bars on the weekend. People thought he was the best at speaking the both the language of medicine and the language of the gay kingdom. There was concern that some of the candidates did not have the flamboyant self-promotional skills that the position required. Many had not produced enough entertaining research on HIV.

The AGP's rehabilitation was painful and slow. He had great difficulty talking, so it was easier to put a pencil in his mouth and have him write out what he was trying to say. Since Peter was the last image he saw before his stroke, much of what he wrote was about Peter. He had been told not to upset himself because that made things even worse. But somehow, he could not get a grip. One day in what was supposed to be the middle of his recovery, pen in mouth, he awkwardly etched two sentences on paper, and then had a second stroke. The words were not easy to read, but as near as anybody could tell they were, "His ass is grass," and "Keep him away from the Blacks."

June

June has always been a very special month for gay, lesbian, bisexual, and transgender brides. It is a favorite month for tying the lavender knot, even if the knot would only be recognized in San Francisco. Gay bridal registries were set up in all of New York City's major department stores and pharmacies. It is also the month that the modern gay rights movement was born, without which there would be no AIDS Empire.

The last Sunday of the month had, since the Stonewall Riots of 1969, become the virtual Christmas and New Year's Eve of the gay kingdom. It was a time to celebrate one's coming out and the tremendous political progress of gay people in America. It was a day to wear a wig and a dress, or nothing at all, as a way of showing your fellow American citizens that you were just folks.

And in no month did the American people show their respect and affection for gays and lesbians like that June. In Washington hearings were being held on the Defense of Marriage Act, which would have outlawed recognition of gay marriages. President William Jefferson Clinton, who had already succeeded in doing the impossible by making things worse for gays in the military, had vowed to sign the bill if it was passed. In a minority opinion on a Supreme Court Decision regarding gay civil rights in Colorado, Justice Antonin Scalia seemed to be arguing that gays and lesbian could be relegated to outlaw status if the good people of America were in the right mood to do so. The Speaker of the House, Newt Gingrich, announced that if his lesbian sister were to marry, he would not attend the wedding. The demand was so great that Hallmark was considering launching a line of special cards for relatives who were declining gay and lesbian wedding invitations.

Behind the scene, the AIDS activists were doing everything they could to follow the stricken AGP's admonition to keep Peter away

68

from the Blacks. They sent AIDS activists to bars in an attempt to distract the Black gay, lesbian, bisexual and transgender community's attention from Peter. It was no easy task, but luckily, most bars in New York were not very integrated and thus far there had been no reported sightings of Blacks in Peter's vicinity. Their biggest concern was that Peter not learn about Project Nurse Rivers, which they considered to be the key to the expansion of the AIDS Empire into the Black community. Nurse Rivers had been the Black person who assisted the government researchers in the Tuskegee Syphilis experiment, the one in which hundreds of Black men with syphilis were allowed to suffer without treatment or knowledge of their infection, so that the researchers could study the effects of the untreated affliction.

Needless to say, when the Black citizens of America found out about the experiment, they were not happy. Even some white Americans were uncomfortable with it. Not to mention two or three white doctors. There were those who thought that from a political point of view, the experiment could have been conducted more successfully on gay men because their community would have volunteered for it and even held benefits to raise money for it.

The Tuskegee Syphilis Experiment was a huge thorn in the side of the U.S. Public Health agencies. Whenever the AIDS activists tried to get the Blacks to dive in and partake of some of the gourmet treats available in the form of AIDS medications, they met with all kinds of resistance. On top of that, Blacks across the country were speculating that the virus had been created to destroy their race. They were mocked repeatedly in the media for suggesting such a thing, as though the very concept that viruses could be altered was some lost Amos 'n' Andy routine. From the general hilarity that greeted their speculation, one would have thought that there was very little difference between biological warfare and ebonics. Those silly Blacks. So paranoid. What will they think of next? One could never be sure which was funnier, the notion that the government could do such a thing or the notion that it would do such a thing. As with similar issues in contemporary racial politics, the appropriate spokesBlacks were found by reporters to denigrate the very idea of biological warfare. But even the most influential spokesBlacks brought up the Tuskegee Syphilis Experiment, to the AIDS activists' great dismay.

For the AIDS activists, there was not an infinite supply of gays with which to carry out the AIDS agenda, so what would happen when there were no more gays in the AIDS cookie jar? AIDS activists have always been a forward-thinking and proactive crowd. There would simply be no more progress in the AIDS Empire unless they could get the Blacks.

When the AIDS activists weren't trying to fend off rumors in the Black community, they had a much bigger problem to contend with: getting Blacks to take AZT. For some strange reason, Blacks could really smell the coffee on this one. They totally distrusted the treatment, and the word on the street was to steer clear of AZT. When reports started leaking out about babies being born with birth defects, like extra fingers and toes, to women who had taken AZT, the AIDS activists did as much damage control as they could. So what if your babies are born with six fingers and six toes, they told Black mothers. Those babies will grow up to be superb basketball players. It's not good enough just to be tall anymore. That campaign had limited success, and the ghost of the Tuskegee Syphilis Experiment kept materializing in a myriad of different forms. At a time when the animal rights special interests were preventing testing on animals, what would happen when the government wanted every Black person in the United States to take an experimental AIDS vaccine? Would the Tuskegee Syphilis Experiment prevent the final piece of the AIDS solution from being put in place?

Thus was Project Nurse Rivers born, a project so secret that it was kept in an underground vault in Greenwich Village beside the original recipe for Quiche Lorraine. There was only one copy of the plan, and all the AIDS activists assigned to the project were strictly forbidden from taking notes during strategy sessions.

Project Nurse Rivers was a project so ambitious that it reached all the way up into the White House. It was the last master stroke of the Avuncular Gay Physician before he had his own master stroke. The plan called for the AIDS activists to lobby the President of the United States to apologize to all Black Americans for the Tuskegee Syphilis Experiment on national television, and to cry while he was doing it. They even wanted the President to throw himself on the ground and weep at the feet of one of the survivors of the experiment and beg for his forgiveness, but they thought this might be a bit much for television. They were convinced, however, that once Black Americans heard the President apologize for Tuskegee and saw tears in his eyes, they would immediately begin to cooperate with the AIDS agenda that the activists had so assiduously prepared for them: the testing, the toxic treatments, the vaccines, the low-cost funerals, or as one of the concerned AIDS activists put it, the whole AIDS watermelon.

Golden Gays had been trying to recruit Sam for years. The organization was the brainchild of two gay social workers who thought that depressed old homosexuals should be organized out of their depression by depressed younger homosexuals. From the way that Sam looked to people who saw him sitting at the bar, he developed a reputation as the unhappiest homosexual in New York. Needless to say, he did not know that he was unhappy. He thought he was just living. To a social worker, the sight of another person's unhappiness is akin to an outbreak of Ebola. It requires extreme intervention.

Social workers from Golden Gays held regular sweeps of the gay bars for gay seniors and they dragged them back to the Golden Gay Center for organized festivities. The social workers of the Golden Gay Center believed that without spending their final days in pottery classes and group singalongs, old gay people were living meaningless lives. Nothing was more verboten to the social workers at Golden Gays then the image of an old gay sitting at a bar with a drink in his hand. It was like seeing your grandmother in her bra and panties.

Sam had escaped a number of Golden Gay bar sweeps by hiding in the bathroom or feigning angina. That June, because it was Gay Pride season, all the social workers had their quotas raised, so the pressure to round up new oldies was intense. One of the social workers was temporarily suspended from her job because she was cheating by bringing in old lesbians from Philadelphia. Sam was approached with all kinds of sales pitches that month, and he finally succumbed when one lad told him that Sam reminded him of the gay grandfather he never had. Sam decided to settle the matter once and for all, saying "Okay, you guys want a golden gay. I'll

71

show you what a golden gay is."

For over two decades, the Gay Pride parade had grown, from a few thousand to close to a million participants. As the celebrants marched down Fifth Avenue in colorful self-assertion, they constituted a floating Utopia for a day. First-time attendees, newly released from the closet, were overwhelmed by a cornucopia of images and emotions. For many people who had lived their youth and early adult years in some form of quiet desperation, complete with the social slings and arrows and the usual nuclear family challenges to their sanity and spirits, the sight of thousands of their own kind (sort of) was akin to an exile's return to his homeland. It felt like their shadowy status was suddenly changing to full-fledged human beings.

On Gay Pride Day, they could turn a corner in Midtown and be abruptly confronted with thousands and thousands of brothers and sisters and comrades, all of them celebrating, not hiding, their situation on earth. This sight caused many a gay man and woman to feel tears welling up from their toes. The word "liberation" should be spared overuse by being saved and protected, like a fine wine, for a moment like this. They had found The Gay Kingdom of Love.

True wizards that they were, the AIDS activists did everything they could to harness these powerful feelings of freedom and self-worth to construct what they hoped would be next phase of gay life in America, the new world order of AIDS-affirming emotions. If Gay Pride Day was a vast colorful canvas upon which were painted every diverse expression of gay hope and affection, the AIDS activists made certain that the thick dark frame around this ebullient picture was the plague.

Peter came to this event with a divided heart. The part of him that was a young gay man thrilled to the erotic possibilities this scrubbed and buffed and chiseled day intimated. But the part of him that was the AIDS assassin saw a much more sinister parade within the parade. He saw a doomed ship of fools sailing down Fifth Avenue. He saw lambs being led by wolves. He had heard about this magical day from other students at college who had been to New York City over the summer break. To the man, the day transformed these students from people who had tentatively and ambivalently come out, to enthusiastic citizens of what they each described as a veritable gay Tomorrowland. And from the way each one of them described it, you would have thought that Walt Disney had invented Gay Pride day. The parade made most of the students realize that gay life could only be lived (the way they wanted to live it) in big cities. Many of the visitors left New York thinking, at their own risk, that everyone in New York is gay. Overcome by enthusiasm and a vision of a new life, they often overlooked the fact that they were simultaneously now weighed down with AIDS chants in their heads, blood-red ribbons on their lapels and AIDS literature in their arms to be shared with all their colleagues in liberation. Without realizing it, many were headed down a Yellow Brick Road not of their own choosing. The AIDS activists knew exactly where you had to be and what you had to do in order to draft the future cannon fodder of the AIDS Empire.

Peter left the parade that day both alarmed and exhilarated and headed up to Cornelia's for dinner. She could immediately tell that he was agitated, and she promptly opened a bottle of one of her favorite white wines from the Sixties.

"The parade's all over television, Peter. They've been having a field day with it. On Channel Two, they interviewed a gay man with AIDS from the parade. On Four they did a transsexual with AIDS, and on Seven they did an anorexic lesbian with AIDS. They were constantly emphasizing the multicultural and diverse nature of the gay community."

"Thank god they don't just interview stereotypes anymore. Did you finish reading the *Messengers*?"

"Did I ever!"

At the beginning of June, Peter had given Cornelia the twenty issues of the *Messenger* that he had bought since January. Over the course of the month she had made Peter several meals and the *Messenger* had been the constant center of attention.

"Peter, the *Messenger* is not just a gay newspaper."

"It's not?"

"It's the Pentagon Papers. It's the missing fifteen minutes of tape."

More and more, Peter was getting the impression that Cornelia held Richard M. Nixon responsible for the AIDS epidemic. The

Messengers were spread out all over her living room. It was a curious sight seeing them lying there under the watchful gaze of Carl Bernstein, Robert Woodward, and Richard Nixon.

"They've got AIDSgate by the balls! I've been on the phone all week. I've talked to every underground Sixties enclave on my Rolodex. They all think this is the sign they've been waiting for. They all want to come to New York and meet Aquarius."

"Aquarius?"

"That's my code name for you. Isn't it perfect?"

"Aquarius?"

"I've told them all that Aquarius has landed and AIDSgate is the sign."

"What do they all say?"

"Well everyone's a visionary in this crowd. They all say that they're not surprised. Every one of them pretends that they secretly knew that the government was lying about AIDS."

"Why didn't they do anything?"

"Because, I've already told you. It's the Fifties again, darling. Everyone is apathetic. Everyone is afraid of risk. Everyone is too busy sitting around eating bags of low fat potato chips and watching Larry King. The time wasn't right. Aquarius had not come. No one knew about the *Messenger*. AIDSgate had not broken."

"So now that you've finished all of the *Messengers*, what do you think?"

"That's easy, darling, the pigs. The pigs are the key to AIDSgate. You can not have a Sixties without pigs."

"It's pretty intense."

"I'll say. Who knew that there was AIDS in the bacon and sausage. And the cassoulet. Me and my girlfriends are going to have to cut back on the cassoulet."

"Pretty big secret, no?"

"They don't get bigger. The ham eaters of America will be on the front lines of the Sixties! Wait till all the kielbasa lovers find out they've been eating meat from herds that had the same medical problems as AIDS patients."

"They should have been giving AZT to the pigs."

"Peter, they would never do that. The animal rights people would never let them. All this talk is making me hungry. Follow me into the kitchen, Aquarius."

Cornelia prepared them one of her best pork-free casseroles and they continued talking about the *Messenger* and AIDSgate throughout the meal.

After dessert and coffee, Peter asked Cornelia to come with him on a surprise trip across town. He wanted to show her something on the East Side.

"I'm game Peter. I love surprises."

Peter directed the cab to drop them off at 86th and Third Avenue. "Let's walk for a while. I have something very private to tell you."

As they walked up Third Avenue, Peter told her he wasn't in New York just to protest the fact that the government was lying about the epidemic. He took a deep breath and told her that he had come to the city to assassinate the epidemic.

"Oh Peter Aquarius Ramsey Wade. Not my pretty one."

"Yes, I must do it."

"I give you my unconditional love and support, but nothing must happen to you. No one must harm a single beautiful hair on your head."

"Cornelia, this is not a game. Anything can happen. Life is not worth living with these damned lies chaining us all to this evil plague. I must do this. I was born to do this."

"I'll help you in any way I can. I had no idea that you were an AIDS Panther. You're such a gentle person. There are things I can do to help. If necessary, I can get messages through to Angela Davis."

They were approaching 93rd Street and Peter stopped and looked up at the large building which was called Yorkville Towers.

"I read about this in an old *Messenger*."

He looked up at the West corner of the building. "Come over here."

They moved to ten feet from the building which looked like it was thirty or so stories high. "Where are we?" she asked.

"In 1985, after they developed that bullshit AIDS test for that sham of a virus, two lovers who lived on the twenty-fifth story of this building took the test, and after they got the results, they drank two bottles of wine. They shared a shrimp cocktail. Then they tied themselves together at the wrist with rope and jumped. They probably landed just about here."

75

"Oh, Jesus Christ, Peter."

"Happy AIDS Pride Day, Cornelia."

July

July made the AIDS activists very, very nervous. Because Fire Island is still predominantly a white man's game, the percentage of people who were in the gay bars in July who were Black increased dramatically, increasing the risk that Peter would strike up a politically dangerous relationship. The AIDS activists decided upon an ingenious strategy of spreading the rumor among Black gay men that Peter was the rich racist son of a racist southern governor. For a while this strategy worked. Many nights at the bars Peter would look around the room and notice that all kinds of hostile stares were directed at him, mostly from Black men. He wondered if he looked like somebody else who was despised by the Black gay community.

Then one night, as he was sitting and talking with Sam at a bar in Midtown, a Black man approached the bar for a drink and stood close to him. When Peter looked at the man's face, he was startled by the anger that seemed to be directed at him.

"Good evening," Peter said, not knowing what else to say that might take the edge off the awkwardness.

"Good evening, white boy."

"Excuse me?"

"Good evening, white boy," said the man.

The man turned with his drinks in hand and went back to his friends.

"Did you hear that, Sam?"

"He must have had a bad day. Or it's his period. Leave it alone, Peter."

Peter was alarmed. He looked around the room. There were about ten black men in the bar and every single one of them was staring at him.

"Something's up, Sam."

"Curiosity killed the cat, Peter."

"Maybe I'm a little paranoid. Tell me some more about all the fun you're having with the Golden Gays."

In the middle of Sam's description of his golden days with the Golden Gays, another Black man came up to the bar and ordered drinks near Peter.

"Hi," said Peter.

The man said nothing.

"Excuse me, are you confusing me with someone?"

"I don't talk to white racists," the man said.

"Who says I'm a white racist?" Peter asked with alarm.

"Everyone," said the man. "Your father's the most racist man in America."

"Who is my father?"

"That governor in the south."

"That's crazy."

"Why don't you go back to where you came from."

"I came from Colorado. My father is in a forest in the West."

"You can't change your stripes," the man said as he took drinks back to his friends

Peter sat there, incredulous, staring into the rows of liquor bottles lining the back of the bar. In the mirror he could see the source of the problem. A man he had once seen tearing up a copy of the *Messenger* was talking to a group of Blacks. As he spoke to them they were all looking over at Peter with disapproving faces. They were shaking their heads. Peter started getting chills.

"Sam, this is terrible. I can't believe this is happening to me."

"Well, maybe you should get out of the kitchen, Peter."

When Cornelia heard about Peter's Black problem, she was beside herself with political joy.

"Oh Peter, I love it! Dirty tricks!"

"Dirty tricks?"

"It's like lubrication."

"It is?"

"It's like foreplay. You can't have a revolution without dirty tricks."

"Why me?"

"Honey, they know who they're dealing with. You should feel proud of yourself. You've just joined a list of my favorite Americans. Nothing really happens in this country without dirty tricks. You can't be totally sure that the government is intentionally doing something wrong until they start with the dirty tricks. Then they start tripping all over themselves because they never have fully mastered the art of dirty tricks. Or they get a guilty conscience and they just muck things up. But one thing is for sure. Dirty tricks beget more dirty tricks and sooner or later they get caught. And when they get caught, the public starts to get antsy, and before you know it, a grassroots movement is born, an uprising starts, and Voila! The Sixties. Peter, this is just another sign. But don't worry. Mama's got a plan for you. I know from dirty tricks. These Trickie Dickies don't stand a chance. I cut my teeth on this crap with SDS, PBS, and the Weatherwomen. This right-on gal's gonna have to make a comeback."

Peter tried to smile and look determined, but he felt more like a wounded young man than the assassin that he was determined to be.

After the Avuncular Gay Physician's second stroke, the best they could do with him was to teach him to communicate by blinking his eyes. His prognosis was grim, and despite the best efforts of the AIDS activists, word had spread that his grip on the AIDS Empire was weakening every day. The man who had built the huge medical plantation on which thousands of AIDS workers toiled was fading fast. Billions of dollars of dangerous treatments hung in the balance, not to mention the future sexual behavior of America. The very thought of America rolling in the hay again sent shivers down the spines of the AIDS activists. The AGP bravely blinked out orders to the activists, but the handwriting was on the wall. If a new leader was not found, there was always the danger that the gay kingdom would reassert itself over the AIDS Empire, and the legacy of the Avuncular Gay Physician would be but a retroviral castle made of sand.

The AGP was not so far gone that he wasn't able to make one thing very clear about his successor. Under no circumstance should one particular odious individual in the AIDS Empire be considered for the position. This was the single person that he hated more than Peter. And as luck would have it, the most dreaded scientist was at that very moment making every strategic move he could to become the Doctor of Doctors.

Ever since word of the AGP's stroke reached the Sonja Henie AIDS Research Institute, its public relations office had been working overtime. Thousands of press releases were being faxed to every country where there were AIDS patients and AIDS researchers. Every one of them was designed to promote the genius and the success of the Director of the Sonja Henie AIDS Research Center, the Inscrutable AIDS Researcher. The Inscrutable AIDS Researcher was himself directing the public relations campaign from a cellular phone as he lobbied for the position of Doctor of Doctors from behind the scenes all over the country. He was beloved in the corridors of his own institution because he had successfully quashed rumors the previous year that the Sonja Henie AIDS Research Institute was associated with dirty ice-skating money. His acute knowledge of the prestidigitations of retrovirology, pharmacology, mixology and public relations made him a formidable contender for the position of Doctor of Doctors, one which had never before been held by a heterosexual with a slight lisp. Privately, he told people that it was time to get the gays out of positions of power in the AIDS Empire. They had served their purpose, and without them, the country's gays and lesbians might never have trusted the whacked-out science that went into the HIV paradigm. Thousands of gay men might have stayed home and watched *Seinfeld* and never have compromised their immune systems with AZT and its siblings. And the Sonja Henie would have become some backwater cellulite research institute. No, he was grateful, but the AIDS caravan was moving on. Besides, the gay and lesbian physicians whined too much and took too long to order in restaurants. If the Inscrutable AIDS Researcher had to make any more small talk about Bernadette Peters, he would leave the field.

The days of cajoling the gays were about to end. After fifteen years of beating around the bush, doctors like the IAR had convinced Congress, the Pentagon, the White House and Kathie Lee Gifford that traditional public health methods for dealing with AIDS were now in order. Although the IAR was a man under forty, he acted as though he had been there the day the traditional pub-

80

lic health methods had been carried down from Mt. Sinai. The use of traditional public health methods had been the manner in which all past epidemics had been brought under control by rational governments. It was a time-honored approach utilized since the beginning of medicine, and it included such epidemic busters as hanging naked widows from trees, bleeding the sick with leeches, and rounding up the Jews. Fortunately, times change and primitive approaches are abandoned. What progressive medical authority would now suggest rounding up the Jews when you could take the more effective modern approach of rounding up the gays?

Todd Browning's classic movie *Freaks* contains a scene in which the most misshapen of adult birth defect victims gather around a guardian and cling to her plaintively like small frightened children. The Inscrutable AIDS Researcher was always moved when he saw this image because it reminded him of the relationship he had worked so hard to cultivate with the gay community. His AIDS patients were like needy puppies nipping constantly at his heels, begging for the newest AIDS biscuit in the form of some bizarre new treatment he could whip up in the lab for them. Their gratitude was overwhelming. People were constantly thanking him, even on their deathbeds. After they were dead, their relatives were always signing big checks for the Sonja Henie. The Inscrutable AIDS Researcher's excellent relations with this community culminated in an award from the Gay, Lesbian, Bisexual and Transgender Physicians of America. He was named the heterosexual physician of the year and given a bronze bust of Ed Sullivan. The day after he was given the award, one of his young gay research subjects toddled into his office and broke down crying. "You love us so much. You, a straight doctor. You like us, you really like us." The young man sobbed and sobbed in tender appreciation. After comforting the young man and thanking him for his mushy support, he made the patient reassure him that he was taking all of his fifty-five toxic medications at the appropriate times and with the appropriate respect.

In light of his history of dedication to all the gay research subjects across America, the Inscrutable AIDS Researcher didn't just want the position of Doctor of Doctors. He felt he deserved it.

Sam's recruitment into Golden Gays was a big boost for their morale. If they could get Sam, they could enlist any difficult old gay thing in the city. Sam grudgingly sat in the back of the room during most of the Golden Gay group activities. Sometimes he excused himself and made drinks in the men's room with a flask of Scotch that he kept on his person at all times. From the bathroom, he toasted his colleagues who were playing gay, lesbian, bisexual, and transgender bingo in the main room. Whenever Sam got out of hand or became too cantankerous, they asked him to take a timeout in the quiet room where they sent all the uncooperative golden gays. Often, Sam ended up playing poker in the room with the Three Mean Old Lesbians, who also periodically ran afoul of the Golden Gay authorities.

One of the first Golden Gay field trips that Sam took was to see the AIDS Quilt in Washington, D.C. Sam was seated on the bus next to the Oldest Perky Lesbian in the World, a woman named Marti. Marti had enough glee in her for a whole barrel of lesbians. Around her, Sam's jowls literally growled by themselves. Her mere existence made him want to quit Golden Gays. Sam wanted to find her happy pills and throw them out the window. All the way to Washington, she was jumping up and down in her seat like a little kid.

"Cheer up, Sam!"

"Why?"

"'Cause you're not dead yet!"

"Yeah, I know. Some people have all the luck. Wanna drink?"

Marti said that she didn't need to be drunk to appreciate the world. Sam said that he didn't need to be sober to appreciate it. After a couple of belts, as they headed down the Jersey Turnpike, everything looked better to Sam, more like its true self. The social workers watched Sam disapprovingly from the back of the bus. They knew they probably had a seriously delinquent golden gay on their hands.

For some reason, on all the bus trips that the Golden Gays took, their sing-alongs never consisted of classics like "Row, Row, Row Your Boat" or "Ninety-nine Bottles of Beer on the Wall," but rather one old Negro spiritual after another. Gays and lesbians were expected to share the sufferings of all other minorities as if they didn't own enough real estate in that area themselves. Since there were not a whole lot of old gay and lesbian spirituals, there may have been no other choice.

Moved by the songs, Marti turned to Sam and said, "Remember Selma, Sam?"

"No, Marti. Remember muff-diving?"

"What?"

"Oh, nothing."

When they were all standing around the AIDS quilt in Washington, all the old gays and lesbians were moved to tears as they looked at panel after panel that bore the name of someone who had died of AIDS. That is, everyone except Sam, who went off into the bushes and had a little cocktail party with two old gay guys he met from a San Francisco contingent of Golden Gays. The social workers wished that Sam had stayed behind the bushes because when he came out, he dropped a cigarette on the AIDS quilt and several fire companies were required to extinguish the blaze.

August

That August, Peter wondered what the AIDS Empire would be like under a President Dole. Could it be any worse then under President Clinton? Weren't the AIDS activists in control of AIDS anyway? There were days when it seemed like the White House was but a tail being wagged from New York by a bunch of angry men with shaved heads and tattoos.

If the Republican platform was any indication, gay people under President Dole were going to feel a little like Mexican jumping beans. There was not a whole lot of euphemism in the document. The conservative crowd gathered in San Diego was not writing an acceptance speech for the Tonys: "We oppose discrimination on account of sex, race, creed, or national origin and will vigorously enforce anti-discrimination statutes. We reject the distortion of those laws to cover sexual preference." (Peter thought that they therefore should get the lesbians to say that all gay people were actually from Lesbos and make a pitch for tolerance based on national origin.)

Despite the fact that it was August, there was a great deal of thought-provoking cultural activity in the gay community. Peter went to the Sanford Meisner Theater to see *Cute Boys in Their Underpants Fight the Evil Trolls*, which he thought might be about AIDS activists, but it wasn't. An Off-Broadway musical called *When Pigs Fly* opened, and Peter was disappointed to find out it wasn't a reference to AIDSgate.

That month the *Messenger* published a couple of hard-hitting articles on the virus HHV-6, which continued to seem like it was more important in AIDS then HIV. One article suggested that it was the primary destroyer of natural killer cells which were almost completely gone in both AIDS and the Yuppie Flu. Natural killer cells are nice to have because they tend to protect against all kinds of germs and cancer. Another article was about a substance called Ampligen, which seemed to stop the ravages of HHV-6. But no one listened because it wasn't about HIV, the AIDS activist-approved cause of AIDS. And the good news was published in the *Messenger*, which meant that it couldn't be true. Peter couldn't believe this catastrophic stupidity was happening before his very eyes. It seemed the AIDS activists would prefer that everyone on the planet die rather than admit that the *New York Messenger* was getting the whole story right. If the country found out that AIDS was a form of the Yuppie Flu, America would have a Yuppie Breakdown. That would be bad for the economy. And the AIDS Empire.

Spite is a strange thing. While it kills some it keeps others alive. Although he was still fading fast and could feel the Gay Reaper approaching in pointe shoes, the Avuncular Gay Physician hung on by one frayed thread of spite. The AIDS activists dared not appoint another Doctor of Doctors while he still drew a single bitter breath. The AGP still had friends and politically speaking, long nasty arms. The AGP lay in bed torturing himself with memories of the arrogant Inscrutable AIDS Researcher. He recognized the IAR immediately for the manipulator he was. It took one to know one. He was reckless with his promises to the AIDS activists. He promised them better AIDS prevention, more surveillance, stricter behavior modification programs, new treatments, new cures, and, most alarmingly, new diseases. The Inscrutable AIDS Researcher teased the AIDS activists that he had a new disease for the gay community that would knock their socks off. We're talking total shut down and remake of society, he hinted. The AIDS activists were beside themselves with anticipation. Visions of new tests and medical interventions danced in their heads.

Word had gotten back to the Avuncular Gay Physician that the Inscrutable AIDS Researcher was sick of the whole gay and lesbian medical crowd. These people did not understand the complex, finer points of poisoning AIDS patients. The final humiliation came when the AGP learned that the IAR had referred to him as the queen of clap. In a few insulting words the entire AIDS Affirmative Action program in medicine was rolled back. All of a sudden all the important gay and lesbian physicians who had risen to such prominence in the AIDS Empire were but field hands on the back forty of sexually transmitted diseases.

The AGP might finally have given up the gay ghost if he could have been in Washington. For, at that same moment, ten stories beneath the National Institutes of Health in the National Security Council's wine cellar, the Inscrutable AIDS Researcher was undergoing his final grilling from the top AIDS activists, the potentates of the self-appointed Council of Three: Hughie, Stewie and Tooey. The Council of Three was considered to be the most powerful self-appointed cell in all of AIDS activism. This was the true eye of the AIDS hurricane. Whatever Hughie, Stewie and Tooey said became AIDS policy. They were watched by all AIDS activists. People dressed and talked like them. When they adopted the Mason Reese hair style festooned with red ribbons, thousands of AIDS activists did so too. AIDS activists constantly talked about the importance of having AIDS icons for the purpose of AIDS education and awareness. The Council of Three were considered to be the ultimate AIDS icon. Las Vegas had Dean and Frank and Sammy. New York had Hughie, Stewie and Tooey. The Donna Karan organization kept tabs on what Hughie, Stewie and Tooey were wearing, and at one point was thinking of launching a line of jeans called Council of Three for the AIDS affirming lifestyle of the urban gay male.

Nothing got done in AIDS without the approval of the Council of Three. At every press conference when some new bit of quackery was being presented as a major AIDS breakthrough, Hughie, Stewie and Tooey had to be there to give the fraud the AIDS activist imprimatur of excellence and grandiosity. They could strike fear into the hearts of researchers who had millions of dollars of grants. There are many who were convinced that Hughie, Stewie and Tooey were the people who decided that HIV is the cause of AIDS. One thing is certain, if they really had made that decision, they had enough power to enforce it. And did they ever. They made sure that every request for funding for AIDS research avowed sufficient allegiance to HIV. Any scientist who didn't think that HIV was the cause of AIDS soon had the honor of having his name in a little red book that the Council of Three kept close to them at all times. If you had your name in that book and you were an AIDS researcher, you were well advised to open up that little cheese store you had been talking to you wife about for years. Even if you just said "Human Immunodeficiency Virus" without enough reverence or awe, you could find your name in that little red book.

If the Inscrutable AIDS Researcher were to rise to the throne of Doctor of Doctors, he would have to meet the approval Council of Three. As the four of them sat in lotus positions on the floor of the wine cellar, the Council members were throwing bitchy scientific hardballs at the IAR. They were not fooling around. The whole fate of the AIDS Empire hung in the balance.

"Tell us your theory of AIDS, Doctor," said Hughie.

"AIDS is one tree clapping," said the Inscrutable AIDS Researcher.

"Very, very interesting," said Hughie.

"How can we conquer HIV?" asked Stewie.

"The moon must talk to the sun," said the Inscrutable AIDS Researcher.

"What about the immune system in AIDS. What is your theory about what is going on?" asked Tooey.

"A sink is full of dirty water, a dead hand is stirring. Time smiles in the wind," answered the Inscrutable AIDS Researcher.

"Wow," said Tooey. "You should have been running the show already."

"Do you think you can totally rid the body of HIV?" asked Hughie.

"A train must devour the butterfly."

"Yes!" said Hughie. "You understand this epidemic better than anybody else." Hughie had a masters in the history of glee clubs, specializing in French madrigals, before he became a top AIDS activist and started making biomedical decisions for thousands of gay people. He knew serious science when he heard it. "What I like about you, doctor, is that you don't beat around the bush."

The Council of Three exchanged knowing glances. They hadn't heard such scientific brilliance since the man who stole HIV from the French researchers compared HIV to a hijacked speeding truck. The Inscrutable AIDS Researcher felt confident that he had won his three little gay friends over, but just to be sure, he decided to lay the brilliance on thicker. "Are you sure you don't want to hear my mathematical formula for ending the AIDS epidemic?"

"We didn't want to force you to reveal it before you publish. We know how you scientists always prefer to leak these things to the press before you leak them to AIDS activists," said Tooey.

"Given the high esteem with which I hold the Council of Three, I would like to give you just a bit of the formula."

"Boy, are we honored," said Tooey.

"Nine times three to the third power divided by four hundred and twenty-three to the tenth power. That's all I feel comfortable telling you right now."

"Those are the numbers we wanted to hear. We now feel certain that under your guidance, AIDS is toast. You do understand the difficult position that we are in. The Doctor of Doctors is clinging to life and we don't want to start a panic in the AIDS activist community by bringing anyone in before he kicks off," said Hughie.

"The night knows its bounds. The dolphin is in the tuna," said the Inscrutable AIDS Researcher.

"Heavy!" said Hughie.

It was Cornelia's idea. She said that they had to fight fire with fire. Peter began going up to every Black gay man in the bars and introducing himself. He told the men that he was in New York to research a book he was writing on the Klan, and he was trying to ascertain whether the Black community was aware that the Klan had branched out into AIDS activism.

He explained to the Black men how he was discovering that the Klan felt that old fashioned mob lynching was bad for their image. Like the move the Mafia made out of drugs and into nail parlors, they thought that the more sophisticated approach of trying to herd Blacks into the AIDS agenda of the AIDS Empire would achieve their traditional aims. They wanted to go mainstream.

Many of the Black gay men said that they had their suspicions about AIDS activism, and they thanked Peter for confirming their sixth sense. They said that they thought that AIDS activists had the whitest gay faces they had seen in a long time. Many of them told Peter that they were going to get the word out about the AIDS Klan, as Peter referred to them. Before long, the AIDS Klan was the talk of the Internet and Black talk shows all over the country. Near hysteria was the response of the AIDS activists. No amount of rumor-mongering about Peter seemed to affect his own rumor-mongering. He was the better looking rumor-mongerer. Besides, what he said turned out to be what the whole Black community seemed to be thinking anyway.

One night late in the month, Peter was lying in bed listening to a late night talk show with a Black host. The host was discussing the AIDS test and how unreliable it was and how the main beneficiaries of its unreliability seemed to be Black people. One of the callers said that he thought the white community was hiding their own AIDS epidemic behind the name of Yuppie Flu and that they were doing all kinds of experiments on so called Black victims of AIDS because they didn't want to try the toxic therapies on themselves. Another caller announced that she thought that AZT was genocide and that she had talked a couple of her friends out of taking it. Another caller said that AIDS was just another Tuskegee Syphilis experiment. Not bad work for the racist son of a racist southern governor, Peter thought.

The pressure increased to make Project Nurse Rivers succeed. The President had to apologize for Tuskegee and soon, the activists felt, or AIDS could deteriorate into some kind of race war. If the Blacks refused to let AIDS researchers experiment on them with vaccines, there might never be an AIDS vaccine. Some of the AIDS activists were so horrified by how quickly the word was spreading in the Black community that they took to wearing T-shirts that said "WE ARE NOT THE KLAN!" That really helped a lot.

On one of the hottest days in August, a group of four men, one handsomer than the next, sat in a table near the window of Angel's Bistro. They all kept their eyes on Peter throughout their lunch. They stayed after most of the diners had finished lunch and left the restaurant. When the room was almost empty, they asked Peter if he would join them for a few minutes. Peter assumed it would be another pitch to join a modeling agency, but it was more exotic. These four men were friends of the Richest Gay Man in America. The Richest Gay Man in America had seen Peter and he wanted to talk to Peter because he was looking for a new escort. His former escort was now in underwear ads sporting a big erection on billboards all over the country. Based on the talent people saw in the ads, he had landed the leading role in the first all gay musical

Hollywood had done in years. Unbeknownst to Peter, the Richest Gay Man in America had seen Peter's picture at an AIDS benefit when an AIDS activist showed it to him as an example of the kinds of hurdles that were facing the AIDS Empire. The rich man hadn't heard much of what the activist said because he was turned on by the photo. He had the kind of discerning eye that makes some men incredibly successful in the fashion business or any other business, for that matter. He knew a star when he saw one, and this face set a new standard. The Richest Gay Man in America, who was used to getting his way, most humbly demanded a meeting with Peter. Money was no object. They asked Peter what he would charge to be the man's escort for one year. Peter just stared at the four for a moment and then after doing some math in his own head jokingly said, "Twenty million dollars."

"We'll get back to you."

September

Perhaps no city in the world was more impressed by the concerns of the AIDS activists than Singapore. The AIDS policies instituted there were so consistent with the philosophy that AIDS is the most important planetary emergency that early in September, one of its gay citizens was seeking asylum in Canada because he was HIV-positive. HIV-positives were never ignored in Singapore and forced to fend for themselves. No genocide of benign neglect could be found there. HIVers were regarded as very special citizens and isolated in the best prison hospitals for people with contagious diseases. Singapore did not just lay back and wait for gay men to be tested for HIV. In many instances, they forced them to take the test for their own good and the good of the other party animals in Singapore. There were no medical slackers in Singapore; every doctor was an AIDS Czar.

In America that warmish September, those who thought that Yuppie Flu (or Yuppie AIDS) was a mild psychoneurotic (nut job) condition, were surprised to learn that euthanasia enthusiast Jack Kevorkian, M.D., had helped one of its extreme sufferers kill herself. If the so-called Yuppie Flu was a fake disease, why were people with it offing themselves?

In Oregon a man who had killed two lesbians was admitting that he murdered them because he hated homosexuals and bisexuals. He expressed no opinion on pre-op transsexuals or vegetarian transvestites. The man was originally just robbing the women, but threw in the slaying for good measure. He told the police that after he realized they were gay, it made it easier to kill them. The man had obviously not been informed of the opportunities in AIDS medicine.

The *New York Times* began a series of reports on the cover-up of the Gulf War Syndrome by the Pentagon, the White House, and the Central Intelligence Agency. As they read the front page story in the *Times*, gay men all over the City breathed a collective sigh of relief. At least there was no cover-up going on about the AIDS epidemic. Thank God that homosexuals had a higher social standing than our men and women in uniform. If only the country's soldiers could organize as powerful a movement as the gays and lesbians, maybe they would command enough respect so that the government would be too frightened to lie to them. And perhaps if the veterans succeeded in their quest to get the government to admit that Gulf War Syndrome is a real, contagious illness, they would become the beneficiaries of the top-drawer scientific research that had been such a blessing in the AIDS Empire.

Say the words "*Pneumocystis carinii* pneumonia," to any doctor in America, and the knee-jerk response will be "gay pneumonia." PCP, as it is affectionately known by the stethoscoped ones, was death's first suffocating hand upon the lungs of AIDS patients. The first case of PCP in 1981 was the seedling from which the entire AIDS Empire grew. It blossoms in human beings when the immune system goes to heaven. What most busy Americans are not aware of is that while it was being considered the telltale sign of AIDS in the early Eighties, the same gay pneumonia, so to speak, was also blossoming in the lungs of our four legged friends on farms all over America. We're talking pigs, here. And unlike the PCP that had been packaged as AIDS in the human sphere, piggy PCP was not limited to pigs who went to broken down motels off the main highway to copulate with pigs of the same sex. No, PCP was not a gay pig disease, or as some AIDS experts would have put it, it was not a disease of fast-track pigs, or pigs who thought that Leviticus was a Marvel Comic book hero.

In the early Eighties, the syndrome that the pigs were suffering from was simply called Swine Mystery Disease. The United States Department of Agriculture had given it this name as if they wanted to confuse the pig AIDS with a third-tier Agatha Christie novel. The hallmark of the disease was a compromised immune system, not unlike the one suffered by the guests of honor in the AIDS Empire. If anyone had noticed a link between Swine Mystery Disease and Gay Mystery Disease, some of the flying buttresses of the AIDS cathedral might have landed like the Flying Wallendas. But the AIDS show had to go on. The only indiscreet entity on earth that publicly noticed the obvious connection between Swine Mystery Disease and AIDS was, needless to say, Peter's favorite deviant newspaper, the *New York Messenger*.

It is a shame that the American people were left out of the loop on this one, for there was a great deal of gastronomic information to savor. How would the more voracious ham sandwich eaters out there have felt, for instance, to know that the ham and cheese submarine they were about to gorge themselves with could have come from a pig that should have been on a respirator with a red-ribboned minister in attendance? The pig might have tried to pass the buck, but surely the cheese hadn't been fooling around.

Pigs hadn't gotten their AIDS because morality had become looser in the pens during the Sixties. The drug revolution had passed them by. They hadn't rejected the values of their parents. Given that their parents were generally slaughtered at six months, their rebellious adolescence lasted about a week and a half. Clearly, sex, drugs and rock and roll did not lead to AIDS in the pig kingdom. It was simply a matter of a virus, and it got around in such a variety of ways that there was little that a condom-bearing busybody pig activist could do about it. And there but for the grace of God went the AIDS activists of the human variety.

After turning Gay America into a nation of supplicating breast-beaters, what AIDS activist in his un-demented mind wanted to hear that pigs all over America had AIDS? How was that even possible? There was no room in the AIDS Empire for sick pigs of the hog variety. You could never hope to get them to wear prophylactics faithfully. Have you ever tried to get a pig to stop oinking long enough to give him a condescending pseudo-scientific lecture on safe sex?

Nothing made the AIDS activists hate the *Messenger* more than the fact that the paper would not let go of the pig story. Over and over the *Messenger* insisted that the pigs had the same disease as AIDS patients and that the government was covering up. And even worse, they published article after article suggesting that pigs were also linked to the Yuppie Flu. How can you build a soup-to-nuts program for behavioral modification in a gingerbread house like that?

How dare the *Messenger* suggest that pigs had AIDS? Had pigs ever summered on Fire Island, or waddled through the bathhouses of San Francisco with a towel loosely tied around a big butt at four in the morning singing about the pig that got away? Well, maybe an occasional pig did. But it was wrong to generalize about all pigs based on the lowlife behavior of a few. It would be hard to sell AIDS in pigs as a gay pigs health crisis. Maybe it was the logistics of dealing with a problem of such magnitude that inhibited the AIDS activists from admitting the truth. There were over 90 million pigs in America, and if all of them had AIDS, how was the Gay Men's Health Crisis to provide them with all the T-shirts, beepers, benefits, buddies, buttons and social services they needed? America only had ten million AIDS social workers and all of them were working on St. Marks Place in Manhattan. And then there was the sensitive matter of experimental treatments. Pigs are notoriously intelligent, considered to be the brightest of the barnyard set. Would they be caught dead taking something like AZT? No way: "Try the hens; do you think we're dead from the neck up?"

And if the AIDS activists had held their noses and admitted that pigs had AIDS, how then were they going to deal with the fact that the Yuppies in expensive designer condoms were also coming down with something that also looked just like the piggy *mal de mud*? That AIDS and Yuppie Flu and Swine Mystery Disease were intertwined and taking place at the same time was a little like an adulterous *ménage à trois* that involved your wife, the milkman and the woman in the wheelchair next door; you really didn't want to know what was happening, and you certainly didn't want to clean up after them.

As far as our government's role in all this, don't we all pay our taxes every year so that government scientists will conceal unpleasant facts like these from us? Which of us would not consider full disclosure in this matter to be a virtual act of treason, an outrageous dereliction of duty?

Cornelia Ramsey Wade had a slightly different take on the American people. While she knew they were dumb, she did not think they were stupid. She believed that occasionally they needed to be awakened by the application of a swiftly swung two-by-four aimed at the headband. Which is why she invited Peter over early one September evening to participate in the opening ceremonies of what she called The Cornelia Ramsey Wade Porcine AIDS Research Institute. She had invited Pat Buckley and Brooke

Astor, but they were no fun anymore. So it was just she and Peter at the opening.

She greeted Peter at the door when he arrived. She was wearing a surgical mask and yellow gloves.

"Are you crazy," he screamed at the sight of her.

"We're going into AIDS research."

"Here?"

"No, in the operating room."

She also had a set of gloves and a mask for him. Once they were gloved and masked, they proceeded into the operating room which was a makeshift effort that incorporated all her kitchen utensils, her large kitchen table, and all her luxurious Upper West Side counter space. On the kitchen table were just about every cut of pork you can imagine.

"I hope you have the stomach for this," she said.

"What are we going to do?'

"I told you. We're now AIDS researchers."

She walked over to the counter, grabbed a package, and held it up for Peter's inspection. It was one of the new home testing kits for HIV. She had bought ten of them, one for each cut of pork. The operation took two hours and they were both sweating by the time enough blood had been collected for each test and the packages had all been secured for mailing the next morning. Throughout the operation, Cornelia kept telling Peter not to treat the meat like it was just meat. "There's a life story behind every cut of pork, Peter."

After they scrubbed up, with visions of Nobel Prizes dancing in their heads, they were ready to do what most surgeons do after a delicate operation like this: drink heavily.

"I'll get the results in four weeks," she said. "There's total confidentiality. Each sample just has a number. Not a single pig's privacy will be compromised. I'll call for the results from a pay phone and I'll use my Woody Allen voice."

"You're really into this pig thing, Cornelia."

"Peter, Mama Cass died eating a ham sandwich. Enough said."

The staff of Golden Gays was so enthralled with the reaction of its seniors to the AIDS Quilt visit in Washington (with the exception of Sam and the Three Mean Old Lesbians) that they decided to organize a Golden Gay AIDS and the Arts Festival. They called the *Times* and the paper decided to run a trenchant series the same weekend about the growing problem of unsafe sexual behavior in people over the age of ninety. All of the Golden Gays refused to pose for a picture that would accompany the piece except for a lesbian who had osteoporosis and severe hearing loss. She didn't understand a single question the reporter asked. She had not had sex in thirty years, but she ended up illustrating a series on the dangers of resurgent hedonism in old homosexuals.

When the piece came out, it focused on the problems elderly people have practicing safe sex if they have arthritis of the hands. Could they really be trusted to put condoms on properly? The right to drive was being taken away from senior citizens in many states. In light of the risks, what about sex? What if the driver of that Volvo that crosses the yellow line and is heading straight toward you is a gay man over seventy with a condom that's only half on?

The *Times* also explored the problems of safe sex and poverty in the elderly. They reported on one old gay fellow who, in addition to being on food stamps, was so poor that he had to re-use his flavored condoms. He was quite the improviser, though. After he washed the flavored condoms he would spray them with Lemon Pledge.

For the state legislatures, the big AIDS fear focused on safe sex in lesbians over 70 with dentures. Were not dentures and latex dental dams a lethal combination, an HIV accident just waiting to happen? Needless to say, the great state of Texas had already led the way on the denture-dental dam issue. If you were a lesbian over 70 with even a partial plate, cunnilingus could cost you twenty-five years in the state pen.

The Golden Gays AIDS and the Arts Festival included AIDS poets, AIDS cabaret chanteuses, AIDS stiltwalkers, jugglers and most entertaining of all, tap-dancing epidemiologists. It was the Cannes of AIDS.

All the old gays seemed to be really enjoying the festivities, especially the AIDS poetry reading. Some of the older women in the front row started crying every time the word "death" was mentioned in a poem. This was especially unfortunate in the case of a poem called "Death in Chelsea," which was a work that consisted of saying the word death over and over, once for each person who had died of AIDS in Chelsea. The poet encouraged the audience to say the word along with him and the poem was threatening to go on for a second half hour when Sam, who had been developing a migraine during the recitation, stood up and screamed, "Get a life, would you!"

By the time the AIDS performance art began, some of the older gays were getting antsy for their Ensure break. You haven't really lived until you've seen AIDS performance art. It is a field that is dominated by ex-accountants. In this instance, the AIDS performance art consisted of a middle-aged man doing an interpretive dance expressing what it feels like to take an HIV test, learn that one is positive, and then find out that one's sister has just become a Rockette. It was a very demanding thing to watch.

After a short break, it was AIDS quilting time. The staff had ingeniously come up with the idea of having each member make a quilt panel of some famous gay person in history who would have died of AIDS had they been alive today. The Three Mean Old Lesbians chose Lizzie Borden. Marti selected Eleanor Roosevelt. Every lesbian over the age of ten was always dragging E.R. out of the closet of the grave. Eleanor Roosevelt has had more lesbian sex since she died than Gertrude Stein had while she was alive. Marti said she thought that Eleanor Roosevelt would have had AIDS because she did everything she could to be close to the common people.

"But she was such a dog," said Sam.

To the staff's horror, Sam made his panel for Abraham Lincoln. "What's he gonna do, sue?" huffed Sam.

Luckily, Sam had spilled so much Scotch on the panel it was never incorporated into the main quilt.

The finale of the AIDS and the Arts Festival was the memoir party. Each golden gay was given an empty black notebook and asked to spend two hours writing his or her life story in such a way that it would help end the AIDS epidemic. It was a lot to do in only two hours, but before long, they were all scribbling away. Some of the oldest lesbians fancied themselves the next Delaney Sisters as they put their lives down on paper.

The president of the gay and lesbian publishing group, the

Pink Triangle Remainders, was on hand to help the neophyte writers. Ever since that organization had been founded, more gay and lesbian novels had been published and remaindered then ever before. "Don't forget to use the technique of foreshadowing," he said. "You might want to remember some trick you had in the Forties, and have that trick say that he has a feeling that something terrible is going to happen in the Eighties. And don't forget recipes. Recipes are very hot in books these days." (One woman took that suggestion very seriously and wrote the first all-recipe pre-AIDS lesbian memoir.)

The staff of the Golden Gays told the scribbling writers that it would be helpful if they would write some guilt into their memoirs as a warning to the younger generation about the AIDS epidemic. It might not be true, but it would save lives. Mentioning the word "guilt" was like selecting a large June bug and asking Sam to put it up his ass. He wasn't having any.

Sam's entries, as laconic as they were defiant, alarmed the staff of Golden Gays. His entry for 1942 was, "I had sex with as many good-looking sailors as I could get my hands on." And his entry for 1943 was, "I had even more sex than in 1942."

This was not what the staff had in mind. One of the younger staff members who was an enthusiastic AIDS activist thought he would take a crack at correcting Sam's vision of life.

"Sam, don't you think that your memoir should express a philosophy that will inspire people to use condoms and get tested for HIV?"

"No," said Sam.

"Well, Sam. What exactly is your philosophy of life?"

"My philosophy of life? My philosophy of life is fuck you."

And with that, Sam was out of the memoir party, and once and for all, out of Golden Gays. To his amazement, the Three Mean Old Lesbians were right behind him.

In the third week of September, Peter watched from his apartment window for the three limousines that were supposed to arrive in front of his apartment at eight o'clock. He had been told that he would ride in the middle car for an hour while he was interviewed by The Richest Gay Man in America.

He had agreed to be blindfolded for the interview so that the Richest Gay Man in America could retain his anonymity. Peter had been told that the man was so rich that he had to travel with more security and hair weaves than a head of state. Peter thought the whole thing was risky and crazy, but he had an idea that could save the world, and it is in such ideas that moral obligations begin to materialize in our souls. For the sake of humanity, he felt he had to pursue it.

Fashionably late, the limousines pulled up in front of Peter's building. The windows were totally blacked out. Peter had been told to walk to the passenger side of the second car and turn around so he faced his building. Two men emerged from the front limo and blindfolded him. For all Peter knew, he might wake up wearing some outrageous costume in some distant land as part of a harem of gay sex slaves.

The men opened the door to the car and protected his head while they gently maneuvered him into his seat and then closed the door.

"You are spectacular," said the person who was seated across from him. Blindly, Peter was face to face with The Richest Gay Man in America.

"Hello," Peter said.

"Thank you for agreeing to wear the blindfold. You're playing fair. That's a good quality. Your pictures don't do you justice."

"Thank you, I guess."

"You make Brad Pitt look like a shoe salesman. Keanu would fall at your feet. You're hotter then Troy Donahue, Leonard Whiting, James Dean and the young Danny Thomas."

"You're very kind."

"So how would you like to be my escort for a year?"

"I really don't like the idea of doing such a thing, but I need the money."

"Twenty million dollars?"

"Yes."

"You're very expensive. You must have a very high opinion of yourself."

"It's not for me."

"What do you mean?"

"I would use the money to buy advertising."

"Twenty million dollars of advertising?"

"Yes. The *Times* is very expensive. I want to run a full page ad every day for a year in the *New York Times*. I figure that would cost about twenty million dollars."

"With what? A picture of yourself?"

"I want to wake up the American people."

"You know, Peter, I was warned that you're not the least bit slutty, but that you are a tad nutty."

"People are entitled to their erroneous opinions."

"What are you going to say in the ads?"

"That the government is lying about AIDS. That there should be all kinds of Congressional investigations. That most of the treatments are killing the patients. That HIV is a huge fraud. That the Yuppie Flu is really AIDS. That pigs all over the country have AIDS and..."

"*Niña, Pinta,* and *Santa Maria*! Are you crazy?"

"I'm not the one who's crazy. Anyone who believes any of this AIDS crap is psychotic."

"You are a trip."

"The whole paradigm of AIDS is a virtual concentration camp."

"Paradigm? That's an awfully big word for a cute little guy like you."

"I'm not little."

"I bet you're not. So you're out to destroy the entire American scientific establishment with a twenty million dollar advertising campaign."

"Let the chips fall where they may."

"Peter, do you know how much money I've given to AIDS research?"

"No."

"It makes your fee look like cab fare."

"I hope you're not proud of that."

"What do you mean?"

"You do realize that you've just helped a bunch of homophobic and crooked scientists play deadly games with gay bodies"

"Says who?"

"Says anyone who isn't in an AIDS trance."

"Peter, have you ever played backgammon with the President

of the United States and then shared a bucket of Kentucky Fried Chicken with him and gotten grease all over the Oval Office?"

"No."

"Look, I'll throw you twenty million dollars, but you can't spend it on anything like that. Nothing political. I can't risk that kind of nonsense being traced back to me. I've worked hard to develop my political connections. I don't need to bring any loose cannons into my life right now. With twenty million, you could buy houses all over the country. You could go anywhere you want to. You could do anything you want. All you need to do is show up at events with me and keep your mouth shut."

"Events like AIDS benefits?"

"Of course."

"I don't want any money for myself. I want to end the epidemic."

"When did you make yourself the Lord of the Plague?"

"I'm just doing what I can."

"Do you know what would happen to me if I was connected to your crazy ad campaign? Do you know what would happen to the gay community if I was associated with that? I shudder to think what would happen to gays and lesbians if I didn't have a good friend in the White House."

"What could happen? Would they force everyone to be tested for HIV and then take AZT?"

"You don't know this, but I worked behind the scenes to get that drug licensed and to get the price lowered so even African American lesbians can afford it."

"On behalf of all the people who no longer have a homosexual in the family to deal with, I thank you."

"Peter, I can have a Chippendale for two years for a quarter of a million and besides, I get a rebate. I think this interview is over."

Peter now knew that he had no choice. He had hoped to accomplish his goal peacefully. Why use assassination when advertising in the *New York Times* could do the trick? No, he had to bite the bullet. He would quit his day job. He had saved enough money to live on for a while. Destiny was awakening inside him. Something was calling him forward, telling him he wasn't just a nice, pretty boy anymore. He sensed he was beginning a journey that would define his presence on earth. The future was dark, the path would be dangerous but something inexorably male that did not involve knowing baseball scores was stirring within him. Peter felt his ancestors gathering in his soul, but this time they were not fighting over money. He was yearning to go right to the center of the AIDS epidemic and kill it. He decided not to shave or wait on tables until the assassination was complete.

October

In October the AIDS activists redoubled their efforts to annex the Black community into the AIDS Empire, despite the growing conviction in the Black community that the AIDS activists were a young offshoot of the Klan. The activists were bolstered by an editorial in the *New York Times* which expressed its concern that Blacks were not availing themselves of all the latest breakthroughs in AIDS treatments because of their lingering concern over the Tuskegee Syphilis Experiment. The *Times* wrote, "Bizarre as it may seem to most people, many Black Americans believe that AIDS and the health measures used against it, are part of a conspiracy to wipe out the Black race...an astonishing 35 percent believe AIDS is a form of genocide."

Also bizarre as it may seem, the words "Klan," or "Paid for by the Klan" were showing up as graffiti on AIDS posters and signs all over New York City. The AIDS activists could barely keep up with replacing their defaced propaganda. Never say that English majors can't have a significant impact upon society.

The city's most inflammatory Black radio talk show host took to beginning his daily program with a joke about AIDS activists. It was a routine often requested by the community and it almost doubled his ratings. A favorite one was: What's the difference between an AIDS activist and a member of the Klan? (The AIDS activists wear red ribbons on their sheets.)

The AIDS activists were terrified that they might have already lost Miami. The largest Haitian radio station there was broadcasting a talk show whose host was urging his listeners not to believe what the government was telling them about AIDS. The host was also warning his listeners not to take AIDS medications because they would kill them. The commentator said that there was not even definitive proof that HIV existed. AIDS counselors, doctors, and numbers runners were apoplectic. To make matters worse, the talk show host had physicians on his show who backed him. They

103

told his listeners that they knew numerous people who had stopped taking the toxic AIDS treatments and were doing very well. Public health officials and AIDS activists were eager to silence the talk show host but couldn't figure how to do so without violating the Constitution. One of the officials said "Everyone has free speech, but this has gone too far."

The concern about this unraveling situation reached the little known room in the White House where the Trilateral Commission was sharing a pepperoni pizza with extra cheese. The Commission decided that it had no choice. Project Nurse Rivers was necessary for the continuation of the Republic. Even though he was tied up with one Penisgate or another, the President would be ordered to apologize for the Tuskegee Syphilis Experiment in order to roll this mess back. If he didn't, Black leaders might start asking sticky little questions about the government's ambitious AIDS vaccine program which they were planning to roll out at McDonalds all over the country.

If you were in the meat section of certain Manhattan supermarkets the second week in October, you were in for a little excitement. No one is quite sure on what day of the week it began, or in which store, but someone was putting disturbing words with blue ink on meat in the pork section of stores all over the city. Somebody was stamping the ribs, the chops, the sausage, the fresh and canned hams with the words, "HIV-positive." Eyewitnesses spoke of a middle-aged woman in sunglasses and a dashiki whom they had seen loitering in the meat section, but nothing showed up on the videotapes. Whoever it was, they were good and they were fast. Stories ran in all the major newspapers, and of course the first suspicion was that some crazed AIDS activist was on the loose and sharing his anger in the meat sections of Manhattan supermarkets. Guards were soon stationed near the ham hocks in several of the affected stores. Thousands of pounds of pork had to be repackaged. At first, the stores considered relabelling all the pork "HIV-negative" and backing it up with an ad campaign utilizing the slogan, "Pork, the other HIV-negative meat." But the big fear was that it would spark an HIV-negative meat war, with the cattle producers arguing that beef is more HIV-negative than pork which, in turn, might lead to the lamb processors hitting back with a campaign insisting that their cuts came from animals who hadn't even had their first French kiss. The Rabbit Council was alarmed that the public would stop eating their cuts of meat, based on studies of consumer fears that most rabbits have something to hide. Not that the Directress of the Cornelia Ramsey Wade Porcine AIDS Research Institute had anything to do with this, but she did receive a very big bouquet of wild flowers from Peter the day the HIV pork caper hit the news.

The AIDS activists knew exactly what was going on. The Gay and Lesbian Alliance Against HIV Defamation considered suing Peter. He had become an out-of-control missionary for the *New York Messenger*. This kid was a walking Chernobyl and nearly every bar in New York City was contaminated. The activists had succeeded in making most of the gay people in New York think that the pig-AIDS link was an expression of homophobia, but now they were hearing it from this sexy latter-day Paul Revere. A damage survey of the bars was sobering. At the Spike, they knew about the mysterious deaths of pigs on farms throughout Iowa. At Kellers, all the talk was about the damaged immune systems of pigs in upstate New York. Down at the Monster, people sat around the piano discussing the lung lesions in the pigs of North Carolina. There wasn't a bar in Manhattan where they hadn't heard about the AIDS epidemic in pigs in one way or another. Gay people were supposed to think, every minute of their brief lives, that *they* were the epicenter of AIDS; *they* were the great American behavioral risk group for AIDS. If *they* were to unify as a people, it was to be one big AIDS sitting duck. *They* weren't supposed to speculate about hams, ribs, pigs, farms, Yuppies, lies, or cover-ups. From a public health point of view, it was not the least bit productive.

The AIDS activists had reached their breaking point. Peter had to be dealt with decisively. The AIDS Emergency Management Act, written for precisely this kind of crisis, had been introduced and passed and signed into AIDS law by the Council of Three at a high level tea dance. A date was set. A deadly but gay-as-a-goose strike force was organized. The lightning-quick hit would be as hard as it was fast. They would fight pork with pork.

The gay bar surveillance division of AIDS activism knew that Peter would be in Splash at 10:00 P.M. on Thursday, October 25, probably being cruised by some stranger and in turn trying to convince the stranger that the government was telling a whopper about AIDS. Peter didn't disappoint them.

At 9:55 P.M., two buses of AIDS activists arrived in front of Splash. At 10:01, over two hundred AIDS activists in pig masks were inside the bar oinking at the top of their lungs.

"OINK, OINK, OINK FOR AIDS," they screamed.

"OINK, OINK, OINK, OINK. ...OINK!"

The sound was deafening. Customers began to flee the bar. Peter had nervously moved to the back of the bar, but the men in the pig masks pursued him, oinking menacingly. One of the activists approached the bar's owner and told him that this was an old-fashioned zap directed against Peter because he was a threat to people with AIDS and all of the values that the AIDS activists stood for. They told the owner that they would not leave the bar until Peter did.

The oinking was incredible. The AIDS activists were surprisingly good at it. The owner guided Peter to the back door and Peter ran for his life deep into the heart of Chelsea. He almost knocked over two bodybuilders who were on the sidewalk pursuing the gay Chelsea lifestyle.

But the oinking didn't stop. The AIDS activists were really getting into it. The oinking took on a life of its own and, almost spontaneously, a second stage of the operation was announced. The pig-faced AIDS activists were divided into groups of four and told to fan out all over the city into all the gay bars. They had gotten rid of Peter. Now they would get rid of the *New York Messenger*.

They grabbed a pile of *Messengers* at Splash and they headed out to every bar in the city and (while continuing to oink) confiscated every free copy of the *Messenger* they could find in the bars. At each gay venue, they went in and oinked warning oinks and waved the *Messengers* triumphantly in the air at the frightened gay customers like the severed heads of an enemy.

"OINK FOR AIDS," they screamed. "OINK FOR AIDS. OINK THE *MESSENGER* OUT OF BUSINESS. OINK THE *MESSENGER* TO DEATH!"

And with that, they vacated the bars and oinked their way down to Christopher Street and they gathered outside the building where the gay liberation movement had been born. A crowd gathered and the street was shut down. They dumped a huge pile of *Messengers* in the middle of the street and after dousing it with gasoline someone struck a match and lit it. Sirens approached the Village from all over the city. Nothing gets the police adrenaline going like trouble in the gay ghetto. The AIDS activists in their pig masks were in a total frenzy. They danced and oinked around the fire. The flames were three stories high. You could see the covers of individual *Messengers* twisting and turning in agony inside the street crematorium. The sight of hundreds of human pigs dancing around a bonfire and celebrating the triumph of the AIDS Empire took the breath away from witnesses at windows in the surrounding buildings. An elderly woman who had been napping awoke in the middle of the commotion, looked out the window, and thought for a second she had died and that hell is a city of pigs. Historians looking for a Kristallnacht of AIDS might be tempted to select this evening as the closest thing. When Peter later heard about the bonfire of the *Messengers* and the wild oinking and dancing, he told Cornelia that this was further proof that AIDS activism was some human form of mad pig disease.

Sam was so angry about what he had seen and heard at Golden Gays that he felt like he was sixty-five again. With his newly discovered energy, in the back of the oldest gay bar in Greenwich Village, he founded an organization to counter the Golden Gays. It would be a true celebration of people like Sam. It would be called Cranky Old Gays. And in honor of his loyal friends, it would have a sister organization called Mean Old Lesbians.

The charter of Cranky Old Gays said that they could smoke and drink and eat cheeseburgers as often as they wanted. Thus was born one of the most subversive gay organizations in history. And it all happened spontaneously. Word got around on the senior circuits and disgruntled Golden Gays from all over the East Coast began showing up at the meetings in the bar. Cranky Old Gays was a concept whose time had come.

Peter was very proud of Sam and took some credit for Sam coming out of his shell and showing that anyone could take a stab at changing the world. Sam took charge of developing a mission statement for the Cranky Old Gays. It grew out of his philosophy of life which, as a philosophy, could probably have competed head to head with Marxism, Existentialism, and Have-a-Nice-Dayism. Sam labeled it Fuckyouism. The mission statement of Cranky Old Gays and its sister organization, Mean Old Lesbians, was *Fuck You!* The first thing the organization did was to assert their commitment to Cranky Old Gay Pride and Mean Old Lesbian Pride. Were these people not one of the most maligned and under-appreciated groups in America? What business in the United States could run smoothly without the presence of a Cranky Old Gay or a Mean Old Lesbian? What airline? What software company? What tanning salon? They crunched the numbers. They made the trains run on time. When some unseasoned soul in a business was overcome with *jejune* inspiration and unseasoned enthusiasm, thereby suddenly suggesting some new hare-brained scheme at a staff meeting, the best companies always had a Cranky Old Gay or a Mean Old Lesbian to shoot it down with a simple "Oh, please." Many people are under the mistaken impression that Warren Buffett has become one of the richest men in the country by investing in blue chip companies. Like all calculating business geniuses, this is just a cover story. The real secret of his success is that he takes major positions and holds onto them for a long time in companies that have the highest number of Cranky Old Gays and Mean Old Lesbians.

Late that month, a rather peculiar letter reached the *Washington Post*. It was addressed to Bob Woodward.

Dear Mr. Woodward,
I am writing to you as one of your biggest fans and as the adopted mother of a gay man who has fought valiantly to awaken his people about a terrible disaster and cover-up that is occurring in our land.
For the last twenty years of my life, whenever anyone says the word "cover-up," I immediately think of you and Mr. Bernstein. You two taught us what a cover-up is.
By the way, please forgive me for never writing to thank you for Watergate before.
Thank you, thank you, thank you. Please thank Carl for

me.

It must be a tremendous challenge to figure out what to do after you do Watergate. I sometimes ask myself, what would I do after I brought down a Presidency? I bet you and Mr. B. ask yourselves that every day. Well, have I got a second act for you two!

Nothing was more spiritually healing for our nation than the reunions of Simon and Garfunkel, and Nichols and May. It's time for a reunion of Woodward and Bernstein.

That would be even more exciting than if Miss Diana Ross got off her pedestal and called Mary Wilson to get the ball rolling. If you've heard any of her latest albums, you know whereof I speak.

You're probably wondering, what's this chick getting at?

Let me cut to the quick, Bobby.

AIDSgate. Yes, AIDSgate.

Can you think of anything bigger or juicier?

I'm sure you've already had an intuition that something was terribly wrong with what we've all been told about AIDS.

Well, you were right.

You've probably also thought that the whole HIV story looked a little like Rosemary Woods stretched out at her desk trying to explain how she erased those tapes.

Well, you were right about that too.

And with that nose for news of yours, I bet that the you've been thinking Yuppie Flu had the distinct odor of AIDS.

Bingo.

Yes, Mr. Woodward, AIDS is just a Nastygate waiting to be exposed.

I bet you wondered where all the bad guys in the Nixon White House ended up. I'm not talking about the big fish. We all know where they ended up. I think that when you start doing your investigative reporting, you'll find that all of Nixon's little fish are over at the National Institutes of Health and the Center for Disease Control, just waiting to be exposed by you and Mr. Bernstein.

I bet that you and Mr. Bernstein have been standing

back, not wanting to hog another cover-up. Well, stand back no more. I have been intimately involved with nearly every one of your colleagues in ways that I would rather not put in writing, and based on those experiences, I can tell you that the only investigative reporters in America who have the brains and the balls to deal with AIDSgate are you and Carl.

It's high time for the big Woodward and Bernstein reunion tour!

I know I write on behalf of your fans all over the country when I implore you to make a comeback and to put AIDS-gate where it belongs. On the front pages of the *Washington Post* with this byline: "Bob Woodward and Carl Bernstein."

I must remain anonymous to protect my sources, but I will be writing you with regular leaks, tips and innuendoes about AIDSgate. So that you will not confuse me with any of the nuts who probably write to you regularly, lets just refer to me as "Upper West Side Throat."

With love and affection,

Upper West Side Throat

P.S. I've been seeing Katherine Graham on TV a lot. Please tell her that red is definitely her color.

If there were going to be an assassination, it was not going to be done ass-backwards. The first thing that Peter did other than stop shaving was to try to get organized. He made his first stop at Staples, where he bought all the assassination office supplies that he thought he was going to need. He bought enough pens, paper, paperclips, binders and file folders for several assassinations. Then he went to a junk shop and bought an inexpensive typewriter. It was all very anonymous because he wore sunglasses, he paid cash, and he spoke with an accent. That didn't stop several of the clerks from cruising him.

Then he bought several cans of coffee so he could drink it around the clock and watch his hands shake because that's what assassins do.

At home, he laid everything out very neatly. This assassin was no slob. Since Peter had never been involved in an assassination before, he began to do a great deal of research. His studies led him to one of the most famous groups of failed assassins in history, the group that tried to kill Hitler. Almost as a form of training, Peter tried to picture himself in such a group. They fascinated him, because they had an inkling they were not going to succeed, and yet they went ahead any way. Peter asked his soul if it could do what needed to be done, even if there was a high probability of failure. His soul actually preferred to be asked questions like whether it wanted Chinese or Italian for dinner.

Peter was beginning to grasp the personal sacrifices that had been made throughout assassination history. One didn't just commit an act of resistance or assassination and then head off to a bar to catch a two-for-one special. A group of students called "White Rose" had ended up being beheaded after resisting Hitler, and Peter learned that there had been more than fifteen attempts to kill the Nazi leader, all of which (obviously) failed. Peter tried to imagine what course history would have taken if Hitler had been successfully iced before the concentration camps had been built. He also tried to imagine what his life would be like if the AIDS epidemic had been assassinated fifteen years prior.

Unlike most assassins, who rob gun stores or buy their weapons in states without background checks, Peter proceeded on his mission without leaving his studio apartment. He read everything he could about Nazi Germany and the people who stood up against it, and he simultaneously meditated on his target, the AIDS epidemic. The more he thought about both, the closer he got to the sinister point where they transected: Nazi Medicine. He felt like a man who has aimed his gun and has his target in his crosshairs, but is not quite ready to shoot.

One night near the end of October, Peter woke up with a start. A horrifying, large, hairy claw was coming at him from beneath a stormy sea. The fingernails were blood red and on each nail was etched the number three. It was the middle of the night and it was cold in the apartment, but Peter got up to write something that had suddenly come into his head. In a flash of golden light the words were shining there in the dark. Out of nowhere, the code of the AIDS Empire was broken. He didn't know where it was coming from, just that it was there before him. He stumbled over to a table and reached for a pen. As if he were sleepwalking, he spontaneously wrote down the three secret laws of the AIDS Empire:

One: You must never say that the government is lying about the AIDS or Chronic Fatigue Syndrome Epidemics.
Two: You must never say that any AIDS researcher is racist or homophobic or a bigot or a bad guy.
Three: You must never compare the AIDS Empire to Nazi Germany.

It was cold in the apartment. Peter was shaking in his snow-white underwear. He went into the bathroom to pee and in the mirror he saw a strange hairy young man with wild eyes. He couldn't tell whether the creature in the mirror was terrified or terrifying. He shuddered at the sight of his own intensity. As he got back into bed, he knew one thing: that to assassinate the AIDS Epidemic, he must break all three secret laws of the AIDS Empire.

When Peter awoke the next morning, even though there was a strange gash on his right hand, he felt totally refreshed and at peace. As he looked around the room, it was as though the hundreds of plants had doubled in size overnight. His little studio now resembled a king's garden, and Peter was now the servant of a vision. He calmly walked over to his writing table, picked up a folder, and labeled it "Operation Treblinka."

The main event had begun.

November

It was really a done deal. The Inscrutable AIDS Researcher would become the Doctor of Doctors. But like all done deals in the world of AIDS activism, it had to go through a dog and pony show that even the activists fondly referred to as fake participatory democracy. There would be no AIDS Empire stretching from coast to coast and into 75 foreign countries without the well-maintained politics of fake participatory democracy.

The Council of Three, who were the keepers of the flame of fake participatory democracy, arranged for the Inscrutable AIDS Researcher to appear before a town meeting of the most powerful AIDS activists in the city. Most of their power consisted of jumping when the Council of Three said to jump, but they were all proud to jump.

The meeting began with the somber news from Hughie that the Doctor of Doctors was in his final days of life, and was only communicating with the AIDS activists, who were holding an around the clock vigil, through his digestive tract. "He sends his love to you all from his death bed, and urges you to continue fighting the HIV cause that he dedicated his gay medical life to," said Hughie.

Hughie also said that the Avuncular Gay Physician had urged the Council of Three to select the next Doctor of Doctors so that the AIDS Empire would not be in any danger while he was incapacitated. Like most things in AIDS, this was a lie. He also said that some AIDS activists had recommended that the Inscrutable AIDS researcher be asked by the Council of Three to fill the shoes of the AGP. But since the Council of Three felt that this decision should be left up to the activists who fought for the AIDS Empire on the streets, they had brought the Inscrutable AIDS Researcher before them to humbly make his case for the godlike position and to answer their stupid questions. If they didn't want him to be their scientific leader, they could reject him. Of course, if they didn't want to unanimously approve his accession as Doctor of Doctors, they could vote no, and they could also have their names put in the red books that each member of the Council of Three was carrying. It wasn't only doctors who were terrified of having their names in those little red books. Anybody with his name in those books could find himself cut off from the newest medical treatments (that were positively fabu), and also from invitations to AIDS benefits, which in New York meant having no social life whatsoever. It was a fate worse than death. It was like being told that you had to live the rest of your life in the gay bars on Long Island.

The Inscrutable AIDS Researcher had done everything he could do to prepare himself for this demanding gay audience. He knew that gay people are a difficult crowd to please until you have a drug problem and are making a comeback. Hughie, Stewie and Tooey had coached him on how to open his presentation with just a couple of words to get the crowd going, and he sucked in his breath and said to them: "Oh Mary!"

Well, they went berserk. They screamed and they cheered and they cried and they sashayed. The crowd was out of control with delight. After a minute of pandemonium, he decided to take the crowd with a line that the Council of Three had told him would conquer every heart in the room: "I'm just a Broadway AIDS baby."

They lost it. The response caused hearing loss throughout the room, but they couldn't help it. They all started chanting a cheer they would chant all night. The IAR had never seen souls so beseeching.

"YOU LOVE US! YOU LOVE US! YOU REALLY, REALLY LOVE US! YOU LOVE US! YOU LOVE US! YOU REALLY, REAL-LY LOVE US!"

The Inscrutable one was astounded by the outpouring. He hadn't felt so appreciated since the time he had helped cover up the cases of AIDS in which there was no HIV. This was the real thing. These were his people. These were the patients he was born to experiment upon and rule. In terms any gay person can understand, it was like being a top in a roomful of bottoms. Now he truly knew what love and power were. God Bless America!

The Council waved the crowd silent and the questioning began. One intrepid soul started the evening by asking the IAR if he could explain to the crowd where HIV came from.

The IAR closed his eyes and meditated for a second, as though he were on *Jeopardy*, and then he responded. "The AIDS virus came out of the left nostril of a green monkey without a handkerchief in Tanzania in the eighteenth century after eating a bad banana. Traveling mariachis contracted the virus during sex when they spotted the monkey under their bed and tried to suck its nose after it agreed to join them in some rough foreplay. From there it spread to the Vatican and then made its way along the spice routes in the genitals of the Knights of Columbus. Any of you who have ever been to New Orleans know what happened next."

They were astounded. They had all heard ridiculous explanations about the AIDS virus before, but this one was the best. Now it all made sense. Finally, someone could explain AIDS in a way that silly queens everywhere could understand.

Then one young activist stood up and asked what his program would be if they elected him the Doctor of Doctors. Hughie looked at the young man, thinking "If?" He opened his red book in a threatening manner. The young man looked a little peaked and quickly sat down.

The Inscrutable AIDS Researcher had been dying for that question and he stood up and unveiled a nine-point program he would implement to run the AIDS Empire.

"One: We must stop pretending that the main problem in AIDS is extending the life of the patient. Our main goal is ending the life of the virus. The virus is the real enemy of America.

"Two: We must embrace all the paradoxes of AIDS. Anything that seems simple and clear about AIDS cannot possibly be true.

"Three: We must immediately stop referring to the patients as 'people infected with HIV.' We must ennoble the patients by referring to them as the domestic battleground of the international war against the deadly virus. I understand the psychology of you gay people. I know that you all want to feel like you're on an awards show that's being simulcast in stereo. Each of you should think of your body as being the Iwo Jima of AIDS.

"Four: New adjectives must be found to describe HIV. Too many journalists use the same old words to describe it and the public is getting bored.

"Five: We must ask Congress to supply financing for a museum of homosexual experimentation to celebrate the sacrifices of gay people who have volunteered for bizarre medical experiments. In the coming years there will be even more to celebrate.

"Six: I will urge the President to sign an AIDS non-proliferation treaty with Australia. If Australia can get its scientists to stop saying that HIV is not the cause of AIDS, we'll keep Mariah Carey and Jewel from touring in Australia.

"Seven: As many of you know, the National Institutes of Health has developed a highly accurate saliva test to detect fraud in scientific research. I will ask them to agree *not* to give the test to AIDS researchers because it would take all the fun out of working in the field."

"Eight: We should stop referring to people who die after taking the Cocktail of Cocktails as 'dead people.' We should honor their struggle by calling them 'treatment compliance failures.'"

"Nine: As soon as a vaccine is developed for a strain of HIV which we pretend is the cause of AIDS, I will go on national television and personally pretend to take the vaccine."

The crowd was on its feet. "YOU LOVE US! YOU LOVE US! YOU REALLY, REALLY LOVE US!"

A hand went up in the audience. "Doctor, what is your position on hope?"

"I believe in hope. While I can't pay for a second home on Martha's Vineyard with it, I believe that it is an important ingredient, especially with regard to my new treatment which can cure AIDS."

There was the dead silence of shock, and then slowly a chant began to build. "CURE AIDS NOW CHA-CHA-CHA! CURE AIDS NOW CHA-CHA-CHA! CURE AIDS NOW CHA-CHA-CHA!"

"I can, I can!" the Inscrutable AIDS Researcher screamed at the screaming throng.

Hughie, Stewie, and Tooey exchanged elated glances. The moment of truth had come. The Inscrutable AIDS Researcher would now utter the words that would destroy all the enemies of the AIDS Empire.

"Cocktail of Cocktails," he said. "I can cure AIDS with the Cocktail of Cocktails. I will end the epidemic."

The activists were doing gay somersaults. The media committee members rushed to the phones to plant stories on the front pages of all the newspapers in the city. People formed conga lines all over the room and started chanting, "COCKTAIL OF COCK-TAILS! COCKTAIL OF COCKTAILS! COCKTAILS! COCKTAILS! COCKTAILS!"

The new Doctor of Doctors begged the crowd to calm down and listen. "But it won't be easy. I have proven that the Cocktail of Cocktails will work mathematically. But it will only work for each of you if you understand the math. I will ask the Congress to provide funding so that two mathematicians will be assigned to every AIDS patient to explain the math so that the treatment works. If just one decimal point is wrong in the formula, the whole Cocktail of Cocktails will fail. This treatment cannot fail you, only you can fail the treatment. In closing I just want to remind you that the most important thing is not whether you live or die, but whether we kill the virus. A new day in AIDS is dawning. Let our new motto be 'The patient is irrelevant, stupid.' "

The audience was in tears and near hysteria. All they could do was jump up and down and chant their new mantra. "THE PA-TIENT IS IRRELEVANT, STUPID! THE PATIENT IS IRRELE-VANT, STUPID!" After jotting down in their red books the names of a couple of audience members who hadn't looked enthusiastic enough, Hughie, Stewie and Tooey fixed their hair and their red ribbons and then joined the Inscrutable AIDS Researcher at the center of the stage. They were then all escorted out a side door by a group of lesbian bikers who had volunteered to be the body-guards for the evening. The future of the AIDS Empire had never been brighter.

When the city's biggest lesbian AIDS doctor got wind of the fact that the Inscrutable AIDS Researcher was the probable next Doctor of Doctors, she got so angry that she started throwing gay men around her office. "This is totally unfair. I've buried more gay men than the Metropolitan Opera. I risked my life going up to Harlem, to listen to some really bad jazz and try to convince pregnant Black women to take AZT and I get called two ton Klannie. All for what? This is what I get for a decade of weird science trying to bring retrovirology, toxicology and homosexuality together in one practice. I don't even understand half this stuff. I've even driven in

117

from the Hamptons on Saturdays to prescribe the latest nucleoside analogues for my boys. I've given them all huge lines of secured credit. I'm not taking this lying down."

Her patients cowered in the corner of her waiting room. Some of them were in hot pants and were holding tambourines, which, because they were shaking so much, they were practically playing. For a few seconds the room sounded like it was warming up for an entrance by Donna Summer. One of the brave souls tried to cheer up the doctor by doing a scene from *Gypsy*. She picked up the littlest gay guy in the room and began twirling him around with one hand. "So this is the thanks I get for putting up with you little buggers."

One of the gay men put his tambourine down and fell to his knees with tears in his eyes and said, "Please, doctor, don't be angry. We worship you. We believe in you. We take any questionable medicine you're in the mood to give us. We support you."

When she finally calmed down, she told her assistant to call her lawyer. She was considering suing the AIDS activists for sex discrimination. "God knows they have deep pockets," she said.

When the Inscrutable AIDS Researcher was told of the potentially embarrassing situation, he whispered in the ear of his colleague, "Tell that fat dyke if I hear one more word about this, she'll get a little visit from the state's Drug Regulatory Division to audit her prescriptions for diet pills. And tell her we know all about the Yankee Doodles and the Devil Dogs."

Not another word was heard from the woman.

In some ways, Sam and Peter were a casebook study in how new ideas and trends get started in the gay ghettos of New York City. Farmers wearing Calvin Klein underwear beneath their Ralph Lauren jeans on their tractors in Kansas often stop in their fields to decrack their Calvin's and ask themselves about the origins of the fashion trends down on the farm. We shall now tell them.

New ideas begin with a single attractive young man who wears or says something slightly new or different in a gay bar full of Chatty Cathies. It can be egregiously stupid, but it must be new or different. Within seconds, a chain reaction of fear and desire takes place, not all that different from butterflies suddenly altering the color of their wings on the outer island of some obscure archipelago. Darwin would have called it a stage in evolution. From New York to Saigon, the dominoes begin to fall and the whole gay universe shifts to accommodate the eccentricities of the newest, cutest face.

How many gay men to whom we respectfully refer as post-*poulet de printemps* now put their baseball caps on backwards without knowing the moment it first occurred many gay eons ago, when the newest cutest thing stumbled into a bar inebriated, dropped his cap and put it back on backwards without realizing what he was doing, where he was, or who he later went home with? Now even nuns in Rome wear their baseball caps that way. His Holiness would be horrified to know where this fashion sin was originally committed. If some hot young man were to show up tonight in Charlies with a pair of speedos wrapped around his head, we would know what all the Broadway producers would be wearing on their heads in Cherry Grove next summer.

It was such a neuropsychosociobiological system that allowed Peter to become the Johnny Appleseed of Resistance to the AIDS Empire.

But thanks to Sam we now know that this hierarchy can be turned upside down. The direction of the rapid gay river of change, from young to old, could actually defy erotic gravity and natural law and reverse course. And all at the hands of the sourest man in the world whose mantra was "Reach out and drink somebody's Scotch."

Was there some vacuum in gay life, and were Sam and the Cranky Old Gays/Mean Old Lesbians just at the right place at the right time? Maybe their attitude and their philosophy were just what the pre-millennial gay psyche was waiting for. Whatever it was, it quietly began to spread far beyond the confines of the cranky, the mean, or the old. Sam had started the new age of Fuckyouism in the gay, lesbian, bisexual and transgender world.

Usually, the next thing that happens in situations like this is that the most derivative homosexual city in the world claims to have come up with it first. Yes, tired old San Francisco, which had always said that it never saw an AIDS treatment or policy that it didn't love, instantly declared itself to be the real birthplace of Fuckyouism. By the time L.A. got into the game, it was no longer gay Fuckyouism, but just Fuckyouism. Fuckyouism had met the melting pot. Disney was soon considering a Fuckyou water ride for adults. An angry Camille Paglia immediately wrote an essay showing how the roots of Fuckyouism could be found in her early essays, and she was considering a lawsuit for plagiarism. Stephen Spielberg announced he would make two Fuckyou epics, one Jewish and one dinosaur.

Fuckyouism was soon being passed down through the generations in the bars, like an ancient recipe for gay chicken soup. Fuckyouism was the potential new meat on the bones of a defenseless people who had seemed powerless against the juggernaut of the AIDS Empire. Fuckyouism was practically a new immune system for gay people. Imagine the first time an AIDS activist approached an AIDS virgin in the bars with all the bells and whistles of AIDS prevention and awareness, only to be dismissed with a very polite "Fuck you." It was not a pretty sight.

AIDS medicine and creative toxic experimentation were perhaps the hardest hit by the tenets of Fuckyouism. The silence of an afternoon walk up Central Park West was shattered by a series of "Fuck yous" coming from doctors' offices that lined the avenue. In one consultation after another, patients were saying "fuck you" to doctors who were suggesting new seat-of-the-pants treatments for AIDS.

AIDS propaganda took a real graffiti beating. No sooner had the AIDS activists taken down the posters that had been defaced with "AIDSKLAN PROPAGANDA," than someone else defaced the new ones with "Fuck You," or "Long Live Fuckyouism." Hitler-style moustaches started appearing on the faces of all the celebrities on the AIDS awareness billboards. A slight edginess broke out in some of the AIDS activists, not unlike that experienced by some German soldiers near the end of World War II. What would happen to them if they lost the war and the AIDS Empire crumbled?

The great cultural war that Patrick Buchanan had always talked about may have finally broken out, but not necessarily along the lines that he predicted. The conflict was between AIDS activism and Fuckyouism. A cute young thing and a cranky old thing may have really started something.

The AIDS activists were having cows.

Cornelia was worried about Peter. His hair seemed to be growing from his soul and his soul was on fire. Although the beard had given an earthy quality to his sexiness, she feared the consequences of his living on the edge. Peter's eyes were more deeply masculine than ever before. They were full of the harshest energy she had ever seen in a man. And for god's sake, he was gay. If Peter's body had split in two and Zeus himself had stepped forward, she would not have blinked. His mission made him seem virile and fearless. While she was enraptured by his fierceness and resolve, Peter awakened maternal instincts in her. At the same time that she wanted him to save the world, she wanted to bake him a pie.

She knew that assassination is a lonely business with terrible hours. She wanted to comfort Peter with unconditional love and reassure him that he was not alone in the world. She wasn't as prepared as she wanted to be, but at the beginning of November she invited him over for a preview of AIDSstock.

When Peter walked into her apartment with his new hairy look, Cornelia gasped, "Peter, you are the wildest man on earth."

Cornelia was not the greatest guitar player, but she was certainly better than the kind of people who make a spectacle of themselves at parties by strumming the guitar as background for their prep school stories. She could pick her way through a tune, and she could even vaguely create one. She had spent the month writing the first songs of what she hoped would be the musical legacy of AIDSgate. She had recorded a few of the songs on her four-track recorder and then sent them to the management of Grace Slick, Joan Baez, Joni Mitchell, and Gloria Estefan. She knew that Estefan was a long shot, but she was sure that AIDSstock would bring the whole entertainment community together almost as much as a cut in the capital gains tax.

Cornelia decorated her living room with posters from AIDSstock's much celebrated predecessor. Woodstock always brought tears to Cornelia's eyes because not only had she been there, but she had helped three midwives who were stoned out of their heads deliver a baby by Caesarian section. The baby had grown up to be one of the most conservative young Republicans, but the moment was still precious. Photos of Sly and the Family

Stone, The Who, Crosby, Stills, Nash, Young and Country Joe McDonald, joined Woodward, Bernstein and Nixon in the living room.

Before the concert of her new material began, she clasped Peter's hands and looked imploringly into his mission-filled eyes. "Peter, the story of your plight is circulating among people whom you will never meet. The Sixties underground network has been re-energized and reborn by the prospects of what is coming, thanks to you. They all hate the Yupeoisie and none of them are surprised to find out that the Yuppie Flu is a secret part of the AIDS epidemic. They all agree that when the Yuppies find out the truth, the Yuppie shit is going to hit the Yuppie fan and the Yuppie values of the last two decades will crash and burn. They're all moving out of stocks and bonds into cash. They're preparing for revolts and riots. They want to be psychologically prepared to march and get arrested and have sex with farm girls and drink really bad white wine from a jug. As soon as they receive word from New York, all across the country they're gonna start burning their red ribbons. They don't care if there's a Constitutional amendment against it. They're just gonna do it. They're everywhere. People with the Sixties spirit have even infiltrated the entire Starbucks chain. They're just biding their mocha cinnamon time until the revolution breaks out. Darling, the code word 'AIDSgate' has reached all of them. As soon as pork futures collapse, they're all gonna head for Kent State. I don't want to make you any more nervous than you are, but in their souls, their psyches, their hopes, their relationships, their prayers, and their paisley broken down vans, they're counting on you."

"Thank you, Cornelia. I don't know what I would do without you."

"Now before I begin, I should tell you that I've copyrighted all the material because back in the Sixties, there were so many drugs that nobody remembered who wrote what. This first song is called 'Landing in a Land of Lies.' I wrote it to capture what you must have felt when you first arrived in New York and started to see what AIDS is really all about. Before Tina Turner agrees to do it, I want you to hear my original version. I may go off key a bit, but you'll get the picture."

The pilot said
Everything's under control
That's when the plane began to roll
We looked out
Upon dark unfriendly skies
We were landing, landing
We were landing in a land of lies

The captain swears
Everything is fine
And we tumble and toss
And the people up front
Make the sign of the cross
And we pretend not to hear
The thunder and the rain
And something is ticking
In the back of the plane
This can't happen to us
We're all so rich and wise
But we're landing, landing
We're landing in a land of lies.

The controllers are
Crying and confused
The passengers all feel
Belittled and abused
The stewardess smiles
And tries to tell a joke
But that doesn't help
Because we all smell the smoke.
And we're circling desperately
While another engine dies
And we're landing
We're landing
We're landing in a land of lies.

"That was spectacular, Cornelia. I can't believe you wrote it. I
hope Tina Turner does it."
"She can't continue racing around the stage and doing 'Proud

123

Mary' every night. That girl's gonna have a heart attack. This next song is called 'Get Off the Bus' and I wrote it as a rallying cry to wake up the African Americans to the racism of the AIDS lies. It's a little heavy. But Woodstock wasn't all Karen Carpenter, Peter."

When we all see what
they're doing to us
We've got to get off the bus
Get off the bus.
Who can you trust
When you're filled with disgust?
Get off, get off
Get off the bus.
They say it's for our own good
That's what they always say
When we ask about AZT
They all just look away
We don't have white coats
We don't have a degree
But we all have eyes
That can clearly see
Stop, look and question,
Stop, look and question
Discuss and discuss
And make certain you
Get off, get off
Get off the bus.

"That was very provocative. It should wake up a lot of people."

"I stole a couple of chords from 'Desperado.' This next one is about my vision of the future. It's a little selfish, but hey, if I don't nurture myself, who will?"

"Let's hear it, Cornelia."

"It's called 'Tie My Hair in Hippie Braids.' "

AIDS means pigs
And pigs are AIDS
Tie my hair

124

In hippie braids.

Yuppies are sick
So are their maids
Tie my hair
In hippie braids

The nation will rise
Yes, really rise, my friend
And women of a certain age
Will get some again
Light the joints
Pass the pipe
HIV is just
A bunch of tripe
Hide your gay sons
Lower the shades
And tie my hair
In hippie braids

Beware the test
And all the rest
Nothing is true
In the fraud of AIDS
Tie my hair in hippie braids
Tie my hair in hippie braids

After Cornelia sang a dozen more songs, they were both exhausted from AIDSstock. Before Peter left, Cornelia gave him a present, something she made Peter promise he would wear to the concert when she finally got it organized. (Why did Bill Graham have to be dead?) It was a beautiful silk T-shirt with a giant sword embroidered on the front.

"It's incredibly beautiful, Cornelia."

"It was completely made by Sixties hands. Not a single finger from the Eighties or the Nineties touched that shirt, Peter. I think it says everything we need to say to each other."

The media loved the Cocktail of Cocktails. Overnight it extended and solidified the imperial boundaries of the AIDS Empire. Medicine had seen the future and the future was the Cocktail of Cocktails. Every publication worth its salt and in the pocket of the AIDS activists did a major story. The Inscrutable AIDS Researcher knocked Madonna off cover after cover as every publication tried to outdo the other's Cocktail of Cocktails hype. Covers ran with lines like "AIDS: Is It Kaput?" The Inscrutable AIDS Researcher was portrayed as one of the greatest minds in science since Einstein, Salk and Lysenko. He was invited to the best dinner parties on Park Avenue and every new opening of a Beefsteak Charlies.

Gay men just adored the concept of a Cocktail of Cocktails. Some said that they heard that it was a secret combination of margaritas and daiquiris. Others were sure that it was really a Mai Tai mixed with a vodka gimlet. *Time* hinted that what made the treatment effective was really the horseradish and the Tabasco sauce. It took *Science* magazine three issues just to publish all the mathematical formulas and haikus that went into the Cocktail of Cocktails. Cocktail of Cocktails buyers clubs and support groups were formed. People threw Cocktail of Cocktails cocktail parties. The whole mood of the AIDS Empire changed as gay men began spending their entire days consuming the COC and celebrating the fact that they were going to live forever while sitting on the toilet enjoying the chronic diarrhea that was one of the hidden benefits of the treatment. It gave people some quality time in which to get back in touch with their bathrooms. One party-pooper scientist kept telling people that the Cocktail of Cocktails had destroyed the intestines of mice in a laboratory experiment, but he was soon dismissed as an insensitive nay-saying homophobe who seemed to be trying to equate successful gay men with dead laboratory mice.

Article after article celebrated the fact that the Cocktail of Cocktails killed the virus, and, even if it killed the patient, at least the person had the solace of knowing that they were dying virus-free. The Inscrutable AIDS Researcher had always said that he wanted to turn AIDS into a chronic disease like diabetes. Since, in many cases, the Cocktail of Cocktails actually caused diabetes in AIDS patients, he had done himself one better. Many were thankful that he hadn't said that he wanted to turn AIDS into a chronic disease like leprosy.

What convinced the gay community that the Cocktail of Cocktails must be effective was the cost. A year's supply cost as much as a season's share on Fire Island. You get what you pay for. Anything that expensive had to be better than AZT.

Suddenly, anyone who had ever voiced any doubts about HIV or the arsenal of edgy treatments that it attracted was made to look mighty foolish. They were like the Japanese sushi chefs who were still making sushi on abandoned Pacific islands after World War II was over. Ironically, the AIDS Empire was expanding, even though AIDS was declared over. As a result, the gay community was turning into one big Cocktail of Cocktails happy hour. The word on the street was, party, party, party!

Throughout November, Peter broke the third law of the AIDS Empire. All his assassination research dared to focus on Nazi Germany and Nazi Medicine. The doctors of Nazi Germany were a fascinating lot. No one in Germany seemed to want to know what they were up to and yet they had created one of the most efficient killing machines in history. If you were going to kill a lot of people medically, you had to be extremely sneaky. Not an easy proposition for husky sausage eaters in white coats. You must speak a language that only an elite understands. The Nazis thought that doctors would be the true saviors of mankind. So did the AIDS Empire.

Like the AIDS activists, the Nazi regime tried to create a constant atmosphere of medical emergency. Just as Congress was pushing for a national registry of HIV-positive people, the Nazis tried to develop a national card index of people who had genetic flaws. The Nazis loved lists, and just as in the AIDS Empire, gay men always seemed to be on them.

The Nazis had some great rocket scientists, but you didn't need to *be* a rocket scientist to understand their game. Before the Nazis could conduct their final therapeutic procedures, they needed to terrorize the medical profession into full cooperation. The same thing seemed to be happening in the AIDS Empire. From everything that Peter had read in the *Messenger*, it was obvious that any misguided souls who spoke up against the AIDS Empire soon found themselves on the receiving end of a stream of vilification. If they were scientists, they lost funding or didn't get tenure. Scientists who kept a low profile and thought to themselves that the Easter Bunny was more believable as the cause of AIDS than HIV soon learned to believe passionately in HIV and to write the official AIDS story into all their grant requests. There was so much winking and nodding going on that AIDS began to resemble an auction at Sotheby's. Journalists who challenged the AIDS Empire either lost their jobs or were moved to beats like restaurant reviewing where they wouldn't be so "obsessed." Filmmakers who didn't think that the government was telling the truth about AIDS soon discovered that they were Oliver Stone.

The Cocktail of Cocktails mania terrified Peter and struck him as one big Nazi experiment that could destroy what little was left of the gay community's political immune system. Already state health departments all over America were talking about passing laws and forcing patients— not asking them— to take the Cocktail of Cocktails in order to "protect the public health." Now as for the etiquette of the Cocktail of Cocktails, if you want gay people to take something, you first have to say, "Please, darling, have one, won't you!" It was one thing to be politely offered an AIDS cocktail when you're in the mood for it and another thing to have one forced down your throat by the yellow-gloved Wunderkinds.

It was all too clear to Peter that gay people in America were the problem and the AIDS Empire—from fraud to propaganda to fake diagnoses to toxic treatments to killer vaccines—was the solution. If it wasn't the Final Solution, it was Final Solutionish.

In Germany the sneaky Nazis had camouflaged the mass murder in hospitals all over the country. In the high biotech world of AIDS, the complicated jargon of retrovirology and the pharmaceutical hokey pokey camouflaged the dirty deeds that were being done to hapless, frightened, trusting patients. AIDS medicine was genocide by gobbledygook. Invisible concentration camps lurked behind euphemisms like AIDS awareness, early intervention, drug compliance, and viral load. Peter couldn't get Hitler's words out of his head: "We must act as the guardians of a millennial future and put the most modern medical means in the service of this knowledge." This guy would have really found his stride in the AIDS Empire, Peter thought. He would have been a very successful retrovirologist. He was the original AIDS Czar.

One of Peter's favorite cosmic coincidences between Nazi Germany and the AIDS Empire was the fact that Hitler's euthanasia project was called the T-4 Killing Project. The cells which the officially declared AIDS virus, HIV, was purported to be killing were the T-4 cells. Did Dionne Warwick know about this?

Peter asked himself whether, if he could go back in time, he would have the courage to assassinate a Nazi doctor. Who would? And before you did, would it be ethical for you ask him to take your blood pressure and give you another prescription for Prozac?

Peter didn't think that the HIV death game was all that complicated. You simply told a person who tested positive on an HIV test that was manufactured by Aeroflot that they were going to die, and then, because they tested positive:

One: You could do anything you wanted to them because they were going to die anyway.

Two: When they died from the treatments you gave them, you could just say whoops, it was the disease that killed them.

Three: You could pat yourself on the back for predicting that the patient was going to die in the first place. It made you look like Nostradamus. Then you could move onto the next patient after a quick call to your broker.

How to assassinate this? How to assassinate this?

He paced and he paced. He drank coffee like he owned a plantation in Brazil. His beard was thick and full. His hair was a lion's mane. It looked like someone had given him the $39 prophet cut and set. If you've ever heard about hostile sex, let it just be said that the erotic energy his body was giving off could have heated the Chrysler building. Operation Treblinka was finally in full swing. Peter was angry. It was not the fake anger of the AIDS activists. It was not the mocking anger of a moronic AIDS chant. It was the killing anger of an assassin. And the angrier he got the more violent were the typing sounds that emanated from his apartment. You would have thought his typewriter was a machine gun. As Peter paced and paced and typed and typed, even his golden hair was racing with anger.

December

It was a tableau that shows how much the body craves its own continued existence. The Avuncular Gay Physician lay in bed clinging to life in a near coma, communicating to the outside world only through a three foot section of his digestive tract. A famous television psychic who was internationally celebrated for finding the graves of kidnapped cats on Long Island was brought in to try and understand the last words of the failing Doctor of Doctors by decoding his flatulence. It was a sad moment in gay history.

"This guy's a real fighter," she said. "As near as I can tell he is saying, 'Throw the dead at Peter, throw the dead at Peter.' That's pretty clear, but then he trails off and I get some interference from the small intestine."

It's a little known fact that people with extrasensory perception are able to fart psychically, and it was through this medium that the expert informed the Doctor of Doctors that the AIDS Empire was safely in the hands of the Inscrutable AIDS Researcher.

That did it. The Avuncular Gay Physician belched angrily and left this mortal coil. The weeping and lamentation of the veiled AIDS activists around the bed went on for days. After announcing the death on the evening news, Dan Rather had to be helped from the set. The whole AIDS empire went into deep mourning. Not since Judy Garland had kicked the bucket on the can had anything like it been seen. Even people all over the planet who were incarcerated in prisons for being HIV-positive wept uncontrollably.

The AGP's last words became the stuff of legend. What exactly did, "Throw the dead at Peter," mean? The words were taken to the Council of Three for an interpretation.

Hughie, Stewie and Tooey were the smarty-pants the AIDS Empire could always count on. They knew exactly what the last request of the Avuncular Gay Physician meant.

"The bald AIDS activist is dying, isn't he?" asked Hughie.

"Yes, he's at Lenox Hill in the celebrity AIDS unit," said Stewie.
"And he's doing a ton of media," said Tooey.
"Perfect," said Stewie.
"Let's pay him a little visit," said Hughie.

No one could convince the Bald AIDS Activist who lay in his hospital bed taking the Cocktail of Cocktails that Peter wasn't behind the wave of Fuckyouism that was beginning to threaten the AIDS Empire. It had the potential to tear apart the HIV unity of New York City. The BAA was convinced that the stress of dealing with Peter was why the Cocktail of Cocktails wasn't working for him. Instead of destroying the virus, it was destroying his intestines, and he lay there in a big diaper that had been embroidered by a fellow AIDS activist from the Fashion Institute of Technology with the words "HIV POSITIVE."

The top AIDS psychotherapists were brought into the hospital, but Peter could not be exorcised from the BAA's psyche. It was their most difficult case and they wrote it up for the *Journal of AIDS Psychoneurotranscendentalimmunology*. They argued that the Bald AIDS Activist was suffering from Post Traumatic Fuckyou Syndrome, and they expected to see many more cases of it. The Bald AIDS activist was the first activist canary in the mine of Fuckyouism. His T-cells went south. His B-cells went north. His macrophages went east. His natural killer cells went west. He was like a smorgasbord with no meatballs. It was an immunological meltdown.

The new Doctor of Doctors was rushed to the hospital to personally handle the case himself. He arrived at the hospital with the entire Advanced Mixology Department of the Sonja Henie AIDS Research Institute. The IAR sat at the BAA's bedside, desperately trying to teach the dying man the complicated mathematical mixology behind the Cocktail of Cocktails. Ten blackboards were brought in for the calculations that proved the treatment worked. He stirred the treatment in a shaker himself. Everyone was so excited to be on the cutting edge of AIDS mixology that they didn't notice that when the IAR spilled a few drops, they burned a hole in the linoleum.

The Inscrutable AIDS Researcher was a little annoyed at the

dying man because he just wouldn't concentrate on the math. The Bald AIDS Activist seemed so excited by all the media attention that he was unable to memorize the nearly six hundred equations that went into the Cocktail of Cocktails. If he couldn't remember the numbers, the treatment would be a total failure. The Bald AIDS Activist went over and over the numbers with the Inscrutable AIDS Researcher, but he kept confusing the algebra and the geometry with his lotto numbers. He couldn't keep any of it straight. As with so many of the first patients, the treatment was working, but the patient wasn't. *He* was failing the treatment.

The IAR left the hospital in a huff, saying, "I can't help this queen. He's mathematically hostile. Is he dyslexic or something? I can't help those who won't help themselves."

It wasn't just the mathematics of the mixology of the Cocktail of Cocktails that the Bald AIDS Activist was screwing up, but also the time and manner of treatment compliance. He was supposed to take three hundred and twenty jiggers of the various cocktails. Some were supposed to be taken ever four hours and others every twenty-three and a half minutes. Some had to be taken on an empty stomach and others with caviar and asparagus vinaigrette. It was hopeless.

The BAA wanted in his last days on earth to be surrounded by all the comforts of publicity. He invited MTV to film his last days for its show *Real People's Deaths*. In an event which caught the whole world's attention, he asked the city's top tattoo artists to come in and tattoo every inch of his body with the words "HIV POSITIVE." He wanted to go down in history as the most positive HIV-positive person in history. Robin Byrd filmed the tattooing of his genitals for her porn show on cable. It worked. The Gallup organization reported that HIV awareness rose dramatically all over the country after the tattooing was broadcast nationally.

At 4:23 AM on December 15th, the Bald AIDS Activist, covered from head to toe with HIV-positive tattoos and smiling for the hunky MTV cameraman, finally failed the last math test of the Cocktail of Cocktails.

As agreed upon with the Council of Three, he was cremated at dawn the next day and his ashes were delivered in an urn to Hughie, Stewie and Tooey.

For the AIDS activists, the Black problem was really exacerbated by a television talk show host named Tony Brown, who for years had been challenging the official story about the epidemic on his weekly program. The man was a dangerous heretic. Brown assaulted just about every belief in the activists' sacred tabernacle of AIDS propaganda. He had violated every public health rule by telling African Americans to think for themselves about AIDS. He was continually warning that they were not being told the truth about AIDS. He called AIDS a "scientifically dishonest construct." He warned them that treatments that were being promoted as effective breakthroughs could actually kill them. He publicly mourned the loss of his friend Arthur Ashe, expressing great alarm that the lies and the AZT had killed him.

Brown warned his viewers that the HIV test could be inaccurate as much as 50 percent of the time. The AIDS activists thought he was the most uppity Black in history. He alone might keep the African American community from entering the white-owned promised land of the AIDS Empire. In a panic, the AIDS activists turned to the one institution in America that can be trusted to elegantly and professionally put the lid back on uppity Blacks: Harvard. After all, hadn't the whole HIV hustle begun in the hallowed hallways of the Harvard School of Public Health? Where fraud in science was concerned, Harvard had a long tradition of excellence to uphold.

Harvard seized the opportunity, and an emergency meeting on African Americans and AIDS was organized to denounce all talk show hosts who urged Black Americans not to cooperate with the government's AIDS agenda. Since most African Americans get up each morning and turn their radios on to hear if any new directions on how to live their lives have been issued from Harvard, the hastily called AIDS emergency meeting had an enormous impact.

As the gay community was dancing in the street and taking their Cocktail of Cocktails, many in the Black community were looking on skeptically. They were only too happy to let the white gay boys go to the well first. They weren't in any hurry. While the White House was desperately trying to get them to forget the Tuskegee Syphilis Experiment, they were remembering it all too well. And despite the media triumph of the Inscrutable AIDS Researcher, up in Harlem they were referring to his brainstorm as the

Cocktail of Caca.

The only thing more efflorescent than gay pomp and circumstance is AIDS pomp and circumstance, and the funeral of the Avuncular Gay Physician was one for the books. The mourners came from every corner of the AIDS Empire. They wore their finest activist clothes. They washed their red ribbons and their most threatening T-shirts and they somberly filed into the Church of St. John the Divine. Since investing in the AIDS agenda produced such high-yield returns for the World Health Organization, it picked up the entire tab. The people at the Centers for Disease Control were relieved that they didn't have to take any money from their numerous slush funds to pay for the funeral.

The International HIV Choir came in two buses from Ft. Detrick. Every single scientist who had fudged on a retroviral research paper showed up to pay his respects.

Dr. Luc Montagnier led a delegation from Paris, and for the occasion he brought five new AIDS co-factors that helped make HIV look like it might have something to do with AIDS. He also brought baguettes. In the spirit of reconciliation, his delegation sat with the mourners from the National Cancer Institute, prudently keeping their wallets in the inside pockets of their suit jackets. The French scientists felt that they could be very good friends with the American researchers, as long as the Americans had nothing to steal.

Hundreds of people on AZT were wheeled into the Cathedral where they could see the remains of the man who had the vision and the sense of humor to treat gay people who had damaged immune systems with chemicals that would do even more damage to their immune systems.

The gravity and the politics of the situation demanded that only one man give the eulogy: the new Doctor of Doctors, the Inscrutable AIDS Researcher. It was a milestone in AIDS history. This death was the crossroads between AIDS past and AIDS future. The IAR spoke of how the Avuncular Gay Physician had risen from his humble origins as a simpering and effeminate little boy, and through dedication and hard work had become a simpering and effeminate graduate of the Harvard Medical School. From there he had gone on to become a simpering and effeminate expert on the sexually and culturally transmitted diseases of gays, lesbians, bisexuals, transgenders and their poodles. Out of such expertise was the AIDS Empire built.

The Inscrutable AIDS Researcher said that he would attempt to carry the torch, and that even though he wasn't simpering and effeminate, he did have a slight lisp and he would attempt to cultivate other qualities that would gain the trust of the indigenous gay people of America so that he could lead them into the sunny new tomorrows of the AIDS Empire.

The IAR used the closing moments of his eulogy to provide some hint of the future challenges that lay before them. It was clear that America was about to take a new direction in AIDS. There was a great hush in the cathedral when he announced that the President of the United States had called him before the service to express his condolences and to congratulate him on his important new position. He told the mourners that he and the President agreed that it was time to put the full force of the American government behind the application of traditional public health methods to deal with the AIDS supercrisis. (Historians please note: this is the first recorded use of the term supercrisis.) The President said, what was the sense of having a government if you couldn't force gay people to do things? It was like leaving a Lexus in the driveway.

The President told the IAR that he was ready to commit the federal bureaucracy, the entire military, and Al Gore's foxy daughters to implement the IAR's plan to treat every AIDS patient with the Inscrutable AIDS Researcher's mathematically proven Cocktail of Cocktails treatment. The entire nation had to pull together. Sacrifices would be required of everyone. There might have to be some suspension of civil liberties, but that happens in all national crises. And, so what if HIV wasn't the cause of AIDS? Even the ACLU would not argue that the virus had civil liberties. If gay people had to sacrifice a little more in the national effort, it was because they had more to gain from the AIDS Empire than their fellow citizens.

Many of the mourners were so overcome with grief that they didn't fully understand the import of what the Doctor of Doctors was saying. But anyone there with half a brain would have understood his message: The manner in which AIDS would be handled in America would no longer be avuncular. From now on it would be inscrutable.

Peter had taken the measure of the AIDS Empire. Anyone who did not understand the odds against bringing about its destruction was a fool. If any rational gay man in New York had grasped its essence or its plans for their future, the terror could have instantly driven them into insanity. The Cocktail of Cocktails was the *coup de grace.* The few times that he ventured out to the bars in December, Peter learned just how effective the propaganda was. People were wearing buttons with the picture of the Inscrutable AIDS Researcher. Drag queens all over America were rediscovering the peasant ingenue look of Sonja Henie. People wept openly in the bars because they thought at last they were putting the epidemic behind them. Many of the bars had to raise the volume of the music to drown out the endless beepers that went off all night. So many people were taking the Cocktail of Cocktails that you couldn't get into the bathrooms. *Details* did a cover story on diaper chic in which they described the hot new billion dollar diaper market that materialized overnight for successful urban gay men who were taking the Cocktail of Cocktails. There were jockey diapers and boxer diapers and the daring thong diaper. And you know gay men—there were the inevitable diaper parties. The mayor had started installing Port-o-Sans on every street corner to deal with the new Cocktail of Cocktails lifestyle.

Peter tried to break out of the depression he was feeling about the Cocktail of Cocktails juggernaut by joining his old associates at the staff Christmas Party at Angel's Bistro on December 20th. Angel was shocked at Peter's appearance when he entered the restaurant. The beard and the hair were wild. Since Angel was a bit of a Mr. Take It, he was quite turned on by Peter's decisively masculine new image.

"Nanook of the North, you look fabulous," he said to Peter.

All the waiters were amazed by Peter's transformation. They had all been somewhat annoyed when he left because the tips went down, but the restaurant was still doing well. Some people came by just to remember the first time they saw Peter. The waiters all wanted to know what Peter was doing. Since he couldn't very well tell the truth, he just said, "Oh, I'm doing some freelance AIDS work. I found an agency that gets me part time work as an AIDS medical ethicist. It's neat. I just show up at a hospital and I get to make ethical arguments for forcing people to take AZT or the Cocktail of Cocktails or both. I use a Ouija board."

All his old friends laughed nervously.

"Oh Peter, you always were such a nut," said Angel. "A hot nut, but a nut."

Peter stayed for an hour and drank a great deal of Christmas punch, and was feeling frisky, so he went down to the Village for a nightcap. He hadn't been to Charlie's for a while. After he got there and ordered a drink, he looked around and immediately he sensed that something was wrong. A number of people were staring at him. A couple of them were whispering into cellular phones.

Hughie, Stewie and Tooey felt an incredible sense of loyalty to the Avuncular Gay Doctor. Without him, there would have been no AIDS Empire and without the Empire there would have been no Council of Three. Without him, they would have just been three sniffy little queens who had to whine their way into Broadway openings and second-night movie screenings. The last request from the AGP had been to throw the dead at Peter. The Council had to oblige. Early in the evening of December 20th, they had handed the dead in the form of a golden urn of the Bald AIDS Activist's ashes off to an elite task force of AIDS activists who had been selected from the leather and lace division of AIDS activism. This was a fearless crowd. They populated the roughest S&M clubs and even bravely volunteered to see the next Kander and Ebb musical.

Initially, Peter's beard had confused the AIDS activists' bar surveillance operation, but once they got over how fetching his new look was, they did their job properly and zeroed in on the fact that he was at Charlie's. An advance party with cellular phones and disco shoes that glow in the dark entered the bar unceremoniously. Nobody noticed them. Nobody except Peter.

Peter thought maybe he should go down to the Monster for his last drink of the evening. He was beginning to feel extremely uncomfortable. He got his bomber jacket at the coat check and headed out.

That uneasy feeling didn't leave him when he hit the street. He started to move rather briskly. This wouldn't have been the first time that he felt he was being followed by a dozen or so people in the city.

As a matter of fact, he was being followed by twenty men in complete leather outfits. They were spread out behind him, trying to look like they were not connected. It was a very unusual sight. Peter began moving faster as he made a right down Christopher Street. Halfway down the block, near an alley, he saw another very suspicious group of men in leather coming at him. It was the Village, so the leather per se wasn't what was suspicious. It was the leather hoods and the tassels. Black leather hoods on top of total black body leather with menacing tassels. Peter's heart was in his throat when he turned around and saw the twenty men coming at him in leather in a formation like an S&M football team. By the time he turned around again, they were on top of him. They dragged him into the alley. Dozens of hands were all over him. They pulled his jacket off and they didn't stop there. As he almost went into a state of shock from the cold and the terror, they stripped him down to the very nakedness he had sworn to withhold from the AIDS Empire.

Finally they had his body. What he had not given and would never have given, they took on their own. The last thing he saw as they dragged him to the ground and he felt dozens of leather hands moving over his body like an army of snakes was a giant golden urn with the words "Bald AIDS Activist" written on the side. He went totally numb as they took the top off the urn, overturned it and began spreading the ashes all over him. While they rubbed the ashes as deeply as they could into the most erotic flesh any of them had or ever would touch, they chanted in the AIDS Activist tradition. "CURE AIDS NOW, CURE AIDS NOW, COCKTAIL OF COCKTAILS, COCKTAIL OF COCKTAILS, COCKTAIL OF COCKTAILS!"

The ashes were everywhere and the men were laughing and howling. Some of them were even oinking. The heretic would never be golden again. As Peter lay there being assaulted, he was only a block away from where the bonfire of the *Messengers* had occurred, and there were still ashes all over the Village. There were ashes in his hair and his beard and his eyes. The ashes of the dead Bald AIDS Activist were even in his mouth. This was as intimate as he might ever be with another human being and it was a dead bald AIDS activist. Peter kept trying to scream, and every time he did they slammed more ashes into his mouth. Blood from Peter's mouth mixed with the ashes.

There is something to be said for an increased police presence on the streets of New York, because when a police car passed by he alley, it was enough to scare the leathered ones. Their lookout shouted, "It's the fuzz, girls," and they dispersed like leather bees. Peter lay there naked and sobbing and covered with the ashes of a dead man from head to toe. As trophies, they had taken every piece of his clothing with them. Peter noticed that the moon was full and staring directly down at him in horror.

What would you do if you had just been assaulted and were lying semi-conscious in an alley naked and covered with a dead man's ashes? And what would you do if a naked young man with wild hair and a bloody beard came down the street covered from head to toe with ashes? What if he tried to stop you on the street in that condition, and incoherently attempted to tell you that he had been attacked because your government was lying about AIDS? Would you turn and flee, even if he had come to save the world?

The next day, the phone at Peter's apartment rang every fifteen minutes. Cornelia was getting hysterical. Peter was supposed to have called her the night before because she was going to hear what she was planning for AIDSstock II. He never called, and she knew something was wrong.

When Cornelia and the super entered Peter's apartment, Cornelia was at first relieved that there was no dead body in the room, but then she started weeping uncontrollably. She asked the super to call the police. Cornelia walked over to the table that Peter had been using to work on his assassination plans, but all she found was a poem by Peter called "The Gay Princes of Treblinka." She folded the poem and slipped it into her purse.

Two policemen arrived and the apartment immediately registered in their minds as the den of an eccentric. Had they known that the missing person was an assassin, the piles of books on the Nazis and the newspaper clippings about AIDS on the wall might have made a great deal more sense. Their first thought was that Peter might have been the victim of a pick-up murder. But when Cornelia showed them his photograph they immediately ruled that out, because the victims of pick-up crimes usually look a little more like Uncle Fester than Peter. When Cornelia told them that Peter couldn't have been a victim of a sex pick-up because he was saving himself for when the AIDS epidemic was over, they shot each other knowing glances as if Cornelia should be considered a possible suspect.

Peter's father set out from an office in a large forest in the west to do what too many fathers have had to do, to search for his possibly dead gay son. Cornelia was not surprised that he had the bearing of a king. They wept in each others arms until he sensed that she might be a woman who was out to lunch.

Peter's father did everything he could to get the police to give special attention to his son's disappearance, but within a few weeks, Peter's case had the same status as that of the housewife who wore her dresses backwards and disappeared from Beekman Place after boiling all of her wigs. It wasn't long before the file on Peter moved into a box of unsolved crimes where his data commingled with that of all the strange disappearances in New York City. Nobody knows better that anything can happen on this earth than a New York City cop.

The list of people who wanted to kill Peter might have constituted a small Gay Yellow Pages. The AIDS activists were only too happy to privately refer to Peter's disappearance as a triumph and a warning. There were still rumors about the suspicious death of an African American AIDS activist who had become a mole and began leaking news about AZT to the enemies of the AIDS Empire. But the police at least feigned ignorance about the arcane and kinky politics of AIDS activism. That was a haystack they had no desire to enter in search of a smoking needle.

There was simultaneously another mysterious disappearance that no one bothered to connect to Peter's. Just days after the assault on Peter, the *New York Messenger* mysteriously went out of business. Since these things always happen in threes, one wondered who was next. Meanwhile, neither Peter nor the *New York*

Messenger now stood in the way of the AIDS Empire. One could jump to all kinds of crazy conclusions. The state of mind of the person who wrote "The Gay Princes of Treblinka" was clearly not happy. The Hudson River was not far from where Peter had been assaulted. He had become a dazed, beaten-up creature who was half man and half ash. He could have stumbled down Christopher Street and, given his semi-conscious state, fallen into the water and floated out to sea to dance with all the other drowned gay princes. New Yorkers were always disappearing in one way or another, into lonely apartments or the city's sacred waters.

When Sam heard about Peter, a single tear moved at a stately pace down his craggy cheek. "It figures," he said.

Sam toasted Peter's legacy all night at the next meeting of the Cranky Old Gays. Sam went on being the quintessential gay survivor. God had one eye on the sparrow and the other one on Sam. He just got crankier, and the Three Mean Old Lesbians who had met and become quite fond of Peter, just got meaner. In honor of Peter, whenever any of them came across any AIDS activists, they told them to go fuck themselves.

For days, Cornelia walked around the Village, unable to believe that he wasn't alive. She was unaware that on Christopher Street she herself was walking though the last ashes that touched Peter. At home she wore black granny dresses and went into a major Rose Kennedy period. One of the great mother-son conspiracies of the millenium had come to an end. When she finally got a grip on her emotions, she decided to take Peter's story on the road. She set out to visit every Sixties enclave across the country to tell people that it would take more than a single brave young man to destroy the AIDS Empire. She played the songs of AIDSstock to anyone who would listen and gave a copy of Peter's poem to anyone who would take one. Cornelia spent the rest of her days trying to keep Peter alive in the heart of America.

Appendix

The Gay Princes of Treblinka
By Peter Aquarius Ramsey Wade

Tonight in the darkness
of the plague
I cried out to the
gay princes of Treblinka
and through the
barbed wire of time
their fingers touched mine.

Lies
from all sides
burden
all of my senses
and the gay princes
in the tortured choir
of Auschwitz
sing to me in my dreams.

What are these cold pills
that come from
the white coats with the
strange, distant, desiccated
smiles?

The gay princes of Birkenau
whisper secrets
from German ash to American
red ribbons.

In terror's trance my
brothers follow
and succumb.
In death
their lovers
are everywhere.

From their graves
the gay princes of Dachau
give birth to a single
defiant
golden rose.

In feverish unconscious
sickrooms
the disingenuous
catheterize the
disinherited
and the gay princes of Chelmno
fill the air
with warnings.

At Chelmno
they all wore
stethoscopes.

At Chelmno
they knew the
importance of
traditional
public health
procedures.

The gay princes of Chelmno
know the importance
of being
disinfected.

After the test, the handshake
and the lecture
the beautiful enraptured
sacrificial princes
arrive by train
and disco down the ramp
into the paradigm
where the nightmare awakens.

The gay princes of Ravensbruck
know about trains and paradigms.

The gay princes of Ravensbruck
know about being
inventoried, listed,
registered and treated.

The gay princes of Ravensbruck
understand what
a state of national medical
emergency is.

The gay princes of Ravensbruck
know what
preventive medicine is.

The gay princes of Ravensbruck
know when a knock on the
door is
medically indicated.

I am in their dying arms.
They are weeping
and I am weeping.

They make me the son
of their final words:

*The lesson of this is
not*

*You must
never let
this happen
again.*

That is not the lesson.

The lesson is:

*You must
never let this
even begin
to happen
again.*

About the Author

Charles Ortleb was born in Elizabeth, New Jersey, in 1950. He attended the University of Kansas. For 20 years, he was the President of T.N.M., Inc., which published the *New York Native*, *Theater-Week*, and *Christopher Street*. Ortleb's poetry has been published in several anthologies, and he has authored books of cartoons. Ortleb has written a play called *The Black Party*. As a lyricist, he has collaborated with a number of composers. He is working on a soundtrack for *Iron Peter*, as well as a sequel to the novel. Ortleb lives in New York City.